ROOKIE SEASON

DENVER KODIAKS #4

PIPER LAWSON

Line and copy editing by Cassie Robertson
Proofreading by Devon Burke
Cover design by Qamber Designs

YOU'RE INVITED

to a cozy

KODIAKS CHRISTMAS

December 23-25

LOCATION: TOP SECRET

RSVP

Dress code: snow boots and tinsel

1

SIERRA

TWO DAYS UNTIL CHRISTMAS

"Turn it off! It's evil!"

"Mariah Carey is *not* evil." Nova's aghast voice comes from the passenger seat of the Volvo as she turns to look at me. Her round blue eyes and pink-tipped blond hair do nothing to make her intimidating.

"Then why do we have to defrost her each December?" I shudder. "She cursed us with this song back in the nineties, and every year, it rears its ugly head. Like one of the four horsemen of the holiday apocalypse."

I lunge forward and hit the skip button on the car's entertainment system. "All I Want for

Christmas Is You" cuts out, replaced by "Blue Christmas."

That's more like it.

I shift to get comfortable in the back seat I share with the stack of luggage that didn't fit in the trunk.

"What are the other three?" Brooke asks from the driver's seat.

"Three what?"

"Horsemen."

I hold up my fingers. "Mistletoe. Candy canes. Christmas lights, Clark Griswold style."

Out the window, we pass growing piles of snow lining I-70 on our drive out of Denver. The mountains rise sharply in the distance, the sky a crisp, cold blue thanks to the altitude. It's a paradise so many vacationers flock to. For me, it's home.

"I never knew you were such a Christmas grinch." Brooke's wearing a bright-orange sweater with fur lining the cuffs, her makeup and skin perfect and hair curly and shiny even though we're on our way to the middle of nowhere.

"Not a grinch. The season is overrated. It's a

huge commercial push to spend money and go to parties and—"

"Listen to Mariah?" Nova finishes.

"Exactly." She's getting it now.

Brooke rolls her eyes at me in the rearview mirror.

The three of us are friends. We've spent lots of nights out together, and I lean on and trust both of them. But in one important way, I'm the odd one out.

Nova's married to one of the starting Kodiaks, and Brooke's engaged to another.

That's right—*the* Denver Kodiaks. World champion basketball team.

Me? I'm the team's unofficial bartender.

Because of the "purveyor of alcohol" thing, I'm one of the more popular people who's not employed by the franchise. And sure, I'm friends with the guys and their WAGs. I give them credit for being down to earth, considering the guys on the team make more in forty-eight minutes on the floor than I do in tips the entire year.

I was still surprised to score an invite to this top-secret holiday weekend.

But the girls must have decided I'm close

enough to being a member of this unofficial club to warrant sharing two days and nights of snowy adventures.

"I swear I didn't pack enough clothes." Brooke drums her manicured nails on the steering wheel.

"You have that massive suitcase in the trunk," Nova points out.

"If that was your suitcase, what's this?!" I nod toward another pink bag occupying an entire seat in the back.

"A few shoes and bathing suits."

My brows lift. "Bathing suits? Thought we were going to a cabin."

"It has a hot tub."

I don't remember that from the invite.

I do own a swimsuit. Something I bought on sale, probably wedged deep in my drawer from the last time I had a vacation. If memory serves, it's a black bikini, which makes the beautiful ink I've been acquiring for the last six years pop.

But it never occurred to me I'd be swimming when I was tossing clothes in a bag for two days of glorified winter camping.

"We're going to get up there and find a line of Kodashians, aren't we?" Brooke's saying.

"No way. The guys kept it under wraps."

"Did you see photos?"

Nova shakes her head. "Ryan was close-lipped about it. Barely gave me the coordinates for the GPS. Even Miles couldn't get anything out of him."

Brooke's fiancé is friends with everyone on the team, a guy's guy, so if he couldn't get any info, no one can.

"I wonder what they've been up to given they've been there all day," I muse.

"Probably sitting around waiting for us," Brooke decides.

The road is full of holiday travelers even before we have to slow for Vail Pass. This section of highway can turn from beautiful to treacherous in an instant.

After navigating the last of the roads, Brooke turns the Volvo onto a driveway. "I thought we were going to Beaver Creek?" She peers towards the line of evergreens hiding the property.

We head up the driveway, passing into a

clearing that reveals a cute cabin with a row of cars in front.

"We're in the right place." I nod toward a Range Rover. "Isn't that Miles's car?"

"And Ryan's," Brooke adds, her voice lifting with excitement.

My friend pulls up her Volvo next to the other cars. It's like a luxury car lot. The row of vehicles probably costs more than the house I was raised in.

"Are you excited?" Nova asks, beaming.

"Um, yes. So excited." To be honest, I'm still not sure why I'm here except that I've gotten to know the team, their families, and their significant others while hanging out with them at the bar.

I'm looking forward to a couple days of decompressing, but I hope this isn't the kind of weekend that makes me realize how different I am from all these people.

The car rolls to a soft stop, and I shift out into a foot of snow. Nova squeaks as it invades the tops of her Ugg boots as she runs around to the trunk.

The front door of the cabin swings wide, and a little tan Frenchie bounds out.

"Waffles!" The dog launches himself into Brooke's arms, and she catches him in a way that suggests she does it often. "Hi, handsome," she coos.

"Hi, Princess."

We all look up to find Miles Garrett filling the doorway, his broad smile far from the only million-dollar part of him. The Kodiaks guard is a crowd favorite for his shooting, not to mention that scores of women would kill to have him look at them the way he's looking at Brooke right now.

"I was talking to the dog." She straightens, the Frenchie peeking out from where he's snuggled inside her poofy orange parka.

"Sure you were." Miles doesn't seem perturbed as he reaches for her waist to tug her toward him, tipping her face up so he can drop a long kiss on her lips.

Cute.

Not that I'm looking for a relationship, but their vibe is undeniably adorable. Even for this cynic.

Relationships are tricky for me. Most of my time is spent at the bar, but the people I encounter at work don't really see me, they just see one version of me.

There aren't enough hours to date after work. Even if there were, my idea of a good time does not involve getting dressed up to bat my eyes at some guy who wants to know if I can tie a cherry stem in a knot with my tongue.

Or worse, one who wants to beat me over the head with his Ivy League education and ask questions about what I want to be "after I get bored bartending." Guys either think bartending is hot and wild or some pit stop on a more acceptable career path. I don't feel inclined to explain why they're both wrong.

We head inside and find the rest of the crew.

Clay, Nova's husband, is a basketball legend. He's huge, with the kind of presence that commands attention even without the tattoos covering every part of him.

Atlas is from Latvia. He's the tallest and seems like the quietest until he speaks with his booming voice.

The champion Denver Kodiaks come through Mile High twice a week when they're in town. I should be immune to the room full of extra-tall, objectively gorgeous male specimens.

I *am* immune, I decide as I take a breath.

The hairs on the back of my neck lift an instant before a cocky voice murmurs behind me, "You missing someone?"

I spin, tripping on my bag and dropping it on my toes.

The man standing behind me fills the entire doorway.

Well over six feet of athlete's body, honed in the gym and on the court. He's wearing a Henley, sweatpants, and a Santa hat and holding armfuls of wood.

The hat covers his dark hair, but his sparkling eyes are on full display.

He's ridiculously handsome, with a straight nose and full lips, even teeth and a strong jaw. The shoulders and flexed arms effortlessly hold enough logs to build a second cabin.

He smells like campfire, as though he's come from one rather than about to start one.

I'm sure it's the cold wind blowing in from the open doorway that makes the hairs on my arms lift, not his sheer sexiness.

A shiver runs through me, making my body

tingle in a way that has nothing to do with the Christmas spirit.

He's way too cheerful.

Too cocky.

Too renewed-his-contract-and-looking-for-a-good-time.

If I was trying to remember why tagging along on a winter wonderland escape with the world champion Denver Kodiaks was a bad idea?

It's because the last time I spent the night alone with one of them, we were both naked.

2

RYAN

"That's gotta be enough." Jay surveys the pile of logs in my arms as we get firewood from the stack behind the cabin.

"Never. Keep going." I adjust my stance to better distribute the half dozen pieces I'm holding.

Jay loads me up with another couple of pieces. "So much for a couple days off lifting in the gym."

"You're not lifting shit." My abs flex under the weight.

He brushes off his mittens. "We're here for two days. We really going to burn all this?"

"And more," I promise.

My teammates call me the *Christmas King*.

Okay, they don't yet, but by the time this trip is done, they will.

This is my favorite time of year. It has been since long before I moved to Colorado straight out of college in Kentucky to join the Kodiaks.

It's not every year we get a few days off that line up with the holiday, and I'm going to be the ultimate host. We have two days until we have to be back in Denver for a Christmas game, and we're going to make the most of every second of fun and relaxation.

The crunch of snow under tires has us both looking up.

I walk toward the corner of the cabin and see Brooke's car come into view and park next to mine. Jay's right behind me. He lifts a hand as though he's going to call out, but I shush him.

"What are you doing?" Jay hisses.

We peer around the corner as Nova, Brooke, and finally Sierra get out of the car.

"Welcoming the girls," I respond under my breath.

My gaze locks on Sierra picking up the rear as the girls head for the cabin. Dark hair spills over shoulders that carry way more than their narrowness suggests. A black ski parka extends partway down leggings clinging to toned thighs. Her feet disappear into Docs that stomp through the snow.

She's short. Not as short as Nova, but without heels, Sierra's probably small enough that her head would tuck easily under mine.

Because I think about shit like that.

Sierra adjusts her bag on her shoulder before heading up the stairs to the door.

I start after them.

It's hard to sneak up on someone when you're carrying a hundred pounds of logs, but I don't back down from a challenge.

"Missing someone?" I say when I step inside right behind Sierra.

"Shit!" She jumps and spins, impressively all at the same time. It's a move our offensive coach would line up for playoffs. When she spots me, her round eyes hurl accusation. "What the fuck, Ryan!?"

Sierra's usually behind the bar at Mile High when I see her. I've hung out with her a few times at a team party or with the other girls, but not nearly enough.

"Merry Christmas," I say.

"You give me a heart attack in the next day, I won't live to see it," she retorts, eyes flashing.

Fuck, she's cute. She looks as if she'd like to take a blowtorch to my face.

Unlike most of the women I've met since signing as a pro athlete, the looks she sends me aren't inviting or seductive. They're all laughing, withering, or pitying. On a lucky day, they're all three.

"Hey, Ryan!" Nova calls from where she's pulling back from an embrace with Clay. "Great cabin. I love how rustic it is."

"Yeah, I actually have a bone to pick with you over that," Brooke calls from the kitchen.

Clay grunts. "It's got running water."

I ignore my teammate and tear myself away from Sierra to set the wood down by the fire and brush the crumbled bits of bark off my hands. "It *is* full service. You tell me what you need and it's done."

"Dude, stop offering my fiancée your services," Miles calls from upstairs.

I scored us this cabin in Beaver Creek. Technically, it's just outside the doors of the gated community because I wanted to be unique.

Those houses would be full service, complete with butlers. Who needs that?

Just because we can afford to doesn't mean we should. Part of the charm is being away from the spotlight and close to nature, which is why I was outside getting my own wood from the firewood pile behind the cabin.

"I'll go get the drinks from the car," Sierra says.

My head snaps up so fast. "You need a hand."

"No, I'm fine—"

"Wasn't a question."

I follow her outside, picking up the boots I kicked off at the door on the way, and trail her to the car.

Getting everyone here was the first part of my plan to get the guys to have the best Christmas ever. I wanted us to escape and have time to ourselves without the cameras or scrutiny—to go off-grid.

The bonus was getting Sierra up here with us.

She works as hard as we do. Probably

harder. Her dad's bar is the center of Kodiaks social activity. As long as I've been here, she's held it down. No vacations. No days off.

The dry, funny, take-no-crap angel at Mile High pretends she's seen and done everything in this world.

She barely acknowledges I'm alive unless I'm trying to buy a drink.

Except for that one night she definitely did…

Suddenly, I'm hot despite the cold temperature.

"Your drive okay?" I ask, feeling my way into this conversation with a softie.

"Every person in Denver and their dog was on their way up here." She rounds to the open trunk.

I peer in the back. It's full of bottles and mixers. "You did not disappoint, bartender."

You might expect a team of huge guys to party hard over the holidays, but some of us don't even drink and the rest of us are light-weights because of our training and metabolisms.

"Couldn't leave you high *and* dry."

"An altitude joke in the first ten minutes. I love it."

She passes me the box of liquor. Her hands brush my arms, and a little zing of electricity has my abs flexing on instinct.

"So, what's the holiday cocktail? Donner & Blitzen? Merry Cranberry?" I ask. "Don't tell me you didn't come up with one."

Sierra looks up at me through thick, dark lashes and folds her arms. "Scrooge Special."

"Sounds fantastic."

Her little laugh is surprised and delightful and totally un-Sierra.

She grabs a duffel bag from the back and shoulders it before closing the trunk with a grunt.

I adjust the box in my arms. It's light, especially after the wood from earlier, but it's also my job to work out twenty hours a week. It's not ego to say that I'm strong and it shows—it's fact.

Sierra doesn't spare a glance at my arms as she starts past me.

What the hell?

They're my best feature, as voted by my fan club.

Here's the thing: I'm a good basketball player. A really good one. Less than one percent of guys who play ball seriously get to the pros. I not only made it but was drafted high, started my first season, and won a championship.

We're talking rare air.

The line of people who want my attention at any given point would've blown my mind as a kid playing ball. Team commitments can pale in comparison to media, agents, publicists, and fans.

Being in the big leagues doesn't mean I'm entitled to have women falling at my feet. But I'm heading toward rich, I'm not bad looking, and being fit is basically my job, so it happens.

Sierra looks at me as if I'm a pain in her ass, even after more than a year of knowing her.

"You genuinely don't love Christmas?" I ask as I follow her inside and to the kitchen. Her lack of enthusiasm over the holiday only makes me more intrigued.

"It's commercial and overblown," she calls back.

"I'm not going to argue with you on the

commercial part, but overblown? No way." I set the box on the counter.

She rolls her eyes and sets the duffel on the counter next to the box.

In that moment, I make a decision. I'm not only going to win over the guys this weekend—I'll win her over too.

"I hope I brought enough alcohol." Sierra takes a quick head count, looking from the kitchen out over the open-concept main floor.

"Unless you're banking on everyone getting their stomach pumped before the game."

"Not happening. I'm responsible."

"Maybe too responsible," I tease, nudging her hip again with mine.

She arches her eyebrow.

A knock on the door has us all turning.

"Hi, friends!" A woman in a furry pink headband and matching parka is standing there with a gift basket as big as she is. "I wanted to bring you a welcome gift and make sure you have whatever you need."

"Kodashian," Brooke mouths to Sierra.

That's what the girls call our female fans. I can't remember how it started, but the name stuck.

The woman's eyes settle on me and warm. "Ryan!" She claps. "Were you outside dressed like that? You must be frozen." She hands the basket off to Miles, who's come down the stairs in time to watch this exchange, and crosses to me. "You're covered in tree."

She giggles as she picks pieces of bark off my shirt. The sound doesn't affect me like Sierra's laugh, but I'm also not a complete dick.

"Uh, guys, this is Trista. She owns the cabin."

When I reached out to book the place, she was only too happy to help. Maybe I should have emphasized how this was a team retreat and that we wanted privacy.

Brooke grabs a soda from the fridge, popping the top with relish.

I see Sierra start for the stairs with her bags. I start to call after her to say I'll take them up for her, but our host stops me.

"You guys are going to have the best Christmas. What's your plan?" Trista gushes.

"Decorating, games, cooking, gift exchange, some light karaoke."

Groans go up.

Trista bites her lip. "You have to come

skiing. There's a hill down the road. Plus, the pond outside is cleared for skating. And don't forget the hot tub."

I definitely hadn't. A warm soak that's not in a too-small standard-sized tub is right up my alley.

"Normally, we'd put up a tree, but I wanted to check with you as to what you'd like," Trista says. "We could order you one. Or you can cut one down yourselves."

"Yeah?" The idea lights me up like a little kid.

I've never cut down a tree. Never lived somewhere with trees like this until I moved to Denver.

"You'd make a great lumberjack." Trista's hands find my arm.

A cough comes from somewhere, along with a muffled laugh.

"Thanks for your help," I say.

She blinks. "Any time. You have my number. Call if you need anything. Or stop by. My place is literally a five-minute walk." She points toward the door. "If you come without a coat, I can warm you up."

"Bye, Trista."

She waves and closes the door behind her.

"Oh, Ryan," Brooke coos in a high-pitched voice. "You should come by my place. You have my number."

Chloe weighs in. "Wear your jersey. Or maybe I'll be wearing it."

I grin as I pull bottles out of the box, setting them on the counter. When I glance back, I find Sierra right behind me. "You're not jumping in on this?"

"Nope."

"Right. Insulting me is below your paygrade."

Sierra inspects the bottles and I inspect her. The pale skin and freckles, the full lips and lined eyes, the piece of black hair falling across her face I'd tuck behind her ear if I weren't concerned I'd lose a finger.

"You know you want to say something." I nudge her hip with mine as she comes up next to me.

She shoots a look over the island toward the others, all caught up in conversations and laughing. They're oblivious. At least for the moment.

"She all but announced she wants you to rail her through New Year's."

Her lips press together as she reaches for the box and pulls out items. Bar ingredients, things to mix with. She pauses on the third jar —maraschino cherries.

I can't resist leaning in. "Missed that tongue."

That's when it happens.

Sierra fumbles the glass in her hands. She doesn't drop it, but for a second, I think she might.

Yeah, well, it's about time.

Because Sierra's been acting as though she has an epic case of amnesia, and there's no way I've gotten that hot night out of my head.

Guess it took being here in these cozy mountain quarters to get under her skin.

I'm not about to let it go.

3

———

SIERRA

LAST CHRISTMAS

"Another usual?" I ask Clay.

He nods and I slide a soda over. He takes it in his big, tattooed hand.

It's Christmas Eve and the bar is full. From the moment the Kodiaks poured in, the vibe changed. It always does when they arrive.

It's not their bar, but in so many ways, it is.

"Settle this for us, Sierra."

I look up at Ryan, his bright eyes locking with mine.

"Who played better tonight, me or Miles?"

"You think I have time to watch you play ball?" I answer Ryan. "Some of us have to work."

Miles grins. "Funny, that's what Brooke always tells me." He winks and goes to say goodbye to the rest of the guys.

All the Kodiaks fans light up around the team, and the guys are happy to rub shoulders with the locals who support them.

The line of women who want the guys on the Kodiaks isn't short. Their fans number in the millions. They've gone from an underdog team to world champions. There's something for everyone—Clay's the all-star, Jay's the team leader, Atlas is the big man with the European accent, Miles is the charming guard.

Ryan's the wild card. The cocky new kid I still can't quite get a pulse on.

Hell, right now there are two women eyeing him up.

"Nice decorations," Ryan says, nodding toward the mistletoe over the bar.

"Dad's fault," I say, shaking my head. "I'd prefer not to post invitations for drunk people to kiss me. I guess he didn't think about it because no one tries to kiss *him*."

Ryan laughs.

Mile High is decorated for Christmas with swags along the length of the bar and lights gracing the top of every wall. It's been that way since I was a kid.

Tonight, I'm dressed in a cutesy outfit that's not my usual style, but in my defense, I was distracted when I got ready for work. My little black skirt shows a ton of leg over my knee-high black boots. The strapless purple top pushes up the girls and shows off the ink—a long Tinkerbell trailing star dust down the underside of one arm and a ribbon below my collarbone. I keep tucking my straight black hair behind one ear when I lean over the bar. I should put a ponytail holder in it and be done, but I haven't had a moment to slow down.

If I'm being honest, the mistletoe hasn't caused that many problems. My regular patrons wouldn't hit on me. The odd drunk person does, but they're easy to dodge.

I haven't had a hookup in a while.

I'm due. Overdue, if we're counting.

There's a lot to be said for a mutually beneficial physical relationship. Everyone knows the score, and expectations don't start to get out of scope.

Still, I'm not using some sappy Christmas decoration as an excuse to get snuggly with someone. Especially not a pro athlete I might see again at my family's bar.

"You going to finish that anytime soon?" I prod.

I've been surveying everyone's drinks—it's second nature and my job—and Ryan's been working on that one all night.

"I'm getting there. You trying to rush me outta here?" His eyes dance as he takes me in.

"Rookies don't need to close the bar."

"Not a rookie anymore, Sierra." He flashes a grin.

"Second year's still a rookie," I remind him. That's how first contracts work in basketball.

"How old are you? I bet we're the same age."

His question throws me off-kilter.

"Twenty-three."

"See?"

"I still know more about life than you. Even if you did go six for six from the line tonight."

"You *did* see my game."

But the weight of his attention has me tingling.

I don't need to look at Ryan to know his height stands out even among a bunch of other players. His dark curly hair makes me want to brush it off his face. His firm lips and bright eyes are movie-star riveting. His huge hands are currently wrapped around his glass in a way that shouldn't be distracting but is.

The two women who've been eyeing him and Miles sense their opportunity and descend. I turn away to serve the other side of the bar, hoping I'm facing the other way by the time my eyes roll.

"You were incredible tonight," I hear one of the women say over the music behind me. I deliberately don't turn back, making drinks for everyone on the other side.

I watch this shit go down every night.

"Hello?" an impatient voice calls.

I turn back to find one of the women flagging me down impatiently. "Can I get a tequila sunrise?"

"We're out of cherries," I say. "I can make you…"

But she's already talking to Ryan. The other woman is laughing too.

I put my own spin on a tequila sunrise, making the drink with a flourish.

I push the drink over.

"Where's the cherry?" She stares me down.

"We're out," I repeat.

Her lips, which have enough filler to claim their own zip code, pout. She runs a hand over Ryan's arm. "But how can I show you the tricks I can do with my tongue? We're under the mistletoe."

She nods toward the little white flowers that are actually way closer to my head than hers.

I clear my throat. "Would you like the drink?"

New patrons are trying to make eye contact with me while I wait for her.

Her attention turns back to me, her smile replaced with disgust. "No. You might be able to drink tequila straight, but I need a cherry in my cocktail."

It's not straight, I want to tell her but bite my tongue since I can see that the message won't sink in.

Ryan looks between us. Before I can lean in, he rounds the bar.

"Come on." He tugs me out from behind the bar and after him.

"I can't leave!" I protest. "Someone might do something stupid. Or steal alcohol. Or..."

"Clay's keeping watch," he says without looking back as he pulls me toward the storeroom.

His fingers are huge. I look down in disbelief to see his golden skin over my tattoos. The feeling leaves a not-unpleasant buzz in my stomach.

When we get to the storage room, I hit the light switch from memory.

Tired fluorescents flicker on with a low hum. It takes a second for my eyes to adjust, and when they do, I see Ryan looming over me with an amused expression.

"What the hell?" I demand.

"I figured you might deck that girl. And as much as I'd love to see that, it's easier without fifty witnesses." His grin is slow, and I'm way too invested in how good he looks when he does it.

Attraction ripples through me. Did I have a drink and not realize it? Because the buzz feels as if it's in my chest at first, then everywhere.

I'm the first person to acknowledge that

sometimes you just need to burn off tension, but I don't do it here or with regulars.

Ryan isn't even a regular. He's a starting Kodiak, which would be a thousand times worse.

At Mile High, we're supposedly in the business of beer, but we're really in the business of the Denver Kodiaks. My dad has always drummed that into me. As much as we can hang out and be friendly, they're the product. Patrons don't flock to us for the Miller.

"This is not the day to test me, Ryan."

His eyes soften. "You've never called me that."

"It's your name."

"I know."

Even with the sound of the music and crowd outside, it's quiet in here.

The throbbing ache through my body moves lower, sets up residence in my stomach, between my thighs.

This is stupid. Every woman on the other side of that door would feel the same damn way being this close to a pro basketball player, particularly one who looks like Ryan.

Even if he smells as good as he looks...

"Maybe I do have cherries." I turn away and scour the shelves. I catch sight of the edge of a jar on a high shelf. I pull over a box and step on it.

"Don't even think about it." Ryan leans past me, easily reaching the jar and bringing it down.

With me on this box, we're nearly the same height. We stare at each other for a moment.

"It must be nice to be this tall. You can tell people what to do."

"Something tells me you wouldn't listen." He cocks his head, and fuck me if he doesn't have dimples.

Ryan holds out the jar of cherries and I take them.

"Thanks. I guess we'd better get back there."

He catches my arm again. "You're not taking those cherries out there."

Confusion makes me blink. "Then why did you get them down?"

"So you'll have them tomorrow. That woman doesn't get one."

I'm so focused on the attraction that I'm not

prepared for the tidal wave of appreciation. It catches me completely off guard.

"You're devious," I accuse. "As much as I'd like to tell her where to stick her cherries, if I can save her dropping a shitty review on my dad's bar, I will."

His gaze flicks over me. "Leave that to me."

Surprise rises up. "But how will she show you what she can do with her tongue?" I bat my eyes up at him.

"I'm not all that interested in her tongue." He says it evenly, but his gaze drops to my mouth. "Yours, on the other hand…"

Shoving down the attraction to a man who's hot and willing and funny and within arm's reach on a lonely day is one thing. Keeping both of us above water and fighting this sudden hunger when it's been a long week and he's not only hot but sweet and on my side is another thing altogether.

I shouldn't care. I don't need someone in my corner. I've never asked for it. I'm married to this place.

So why does it feel so damn good?

Then he kisses me, and every thought goes out the window.

4

SIERRA

"How many bedrooms does this cabin have?" Chloe asks.

"Five," Jay calls.

"How many stairs?" Brooke gripes as she drags her suitcase up the stairs.

Miles swipes for her case even though he has one in his other hand. "Remind me why you need all these clothes, Princess. You know I like you better without 'em."

I'm still thinking about Ryan in the kitchen. When I thought about coming up with the team this weekend, I figured I could forget what happened between us last year.

I've done a good job of it the past twelve

months despite seeing him twice a week. Why should that change now?

Turns out seeing him up close in a cozy cabin is a whole different vibe.

Especially when I feel him at my back heading up the stairs.

"I missed your tongue, Sierra."

The words echo in my head.

"So, wait…" I'm trying to catch up, trailing the line of bodies up the creaking plank stairs. "Tell me how these sleeping arrangements are supposed to work."

We make it to the top, my heart thudding a little despite that I spend my days on my feet.

Up here, there's a long hall with doors leading off it on either side.

"I see four bedrooms. Where's the fifth?" I ask.

"Uhhh…"

We go hunting for it but can't find a door to a fifth bedroom.

"You could call Trista," Miles suggests.

"No!" the other girls chorus.

"We'd never get Ryan back," Brooke adds. "If she got her tentacles around him, she'd drag him back to her cabin and smother him."

"Then I guess there're four," Ryan says, shrugging. "Two for the guys and two for the girls."

The hallway erupts.

The loudest protestors are Miles and Brooke, but it's Clay who cuts through it all with a look.

"This is Nova's and my room. Anyone got a problem, don't bring it to me." He shuts the door after them.

"My dude is onto something," Miles says, looping an arm around Brooke's shoulders.

Brooke ducks out to peer in a couple of doorways. "This one has a king bed."

"It's ours," Miles decides.

Ryan's frowning. "It's cool. We'll do a little rebalancing…"

That leaves two rooms with Atlas, Jay, Ryan, Chloe, and me needing beds. I stick my head into a room. "This one has bunks." Two sets. "This for the guys?"

Chloe glances in the other room. "A king in this one, plus a pullout."

"My feet are going to hang over the edge," Atlas complains.

"You've had worse," Jay counters.

We drop our bags, and Chloe squares her shoulders. "I knew I should have taken a day off and gone to the spa instead."

My lips twitch as I watch her unpack on the king bed. "Why *did* you come?"

"To keep an eye on them and ensure they get back to Denver in one piece. The game against LA on Christmas is the biggest one of the year. The rivalry is enormous. Fans are pumped. What are you doing?" she asks as I scope out the pullout.

"I figured you'd take the bed and I'd take the couch. You're on the clock, so you need to get a good sleep."

"That's sweet of you. But we can share as long as you're not aggressive with your feet."

"No promises." Still, I'm grateful not to have to risk it on the pullout.

Christmas music drifts down the hallway.

"Let's go, party people!" Ryan hollers.

A few moments later, we're all gathered back down in the living room where Ryan has hung a small whiteboard that reads: "KOZY KODIAKS CHRISTMAS."

"Now," he begins, uncapping a purple dry

erase marker, "the best Christmas ever has a plan."

"You steal that from Coach?" Miles nods toward the Kodiaks logo in the corner of the whiteboard.

"Pre-Christmas," Chloe reminds Ryan. "Our asses have to be back at Kodiaks arena in"—she checks her phone—"forty-eight hours."

"And ready to tear LA a new one," Jay adds.

"Yeah, yeah." Ryan writes a list, plus draws diagrams.

My brows lift at his thoroughness and dedication. He's sorted out meals, games, movies, a gift swap, and karaoke.

"What's at stake?" Jay asks.

Chloe frowns at him. "It's not a competition."

"It should be."

Ryan huffs. "If this isn't the best Kodiaks Christmas ever... I'll buy everyone a new Christmas tree."

"Nah, too easy. You'll buy everyone a new tree and do team media for the next month."

He blinks. "No way."

"You can't assign press duties like that," Chloe agrees.

"Chlo, here's the thing..." Jay loops an arm around her shoulders, and she raises one brow. "We're competitive creatures, but we need motivation. Come on, Ryan. You don't think you can pull this off?"

Ryan's face screws up. "Fine."

Cheers go around the room. It almost feels like the rest of the team has already won.

"First up, decorations," Ryan decides. "We need a tree."

"How are you going to cut one down?" Jay asks.

"There's a shed out back. Must have tools."

The group of us bundle up and head outside.

In front of the cabin is the parking area and a few trees between us and the road. Behind the building is the hot tub with a pile of wood at one side. There's a clearing with a small shed, plus a path that leads into the woods.

"It's locked," Jay says when we get to the shed.

Ryan curses, yanking on the padlock. "There was nothing up at the cabin."

"Your girlfriend didn't leave you a key?"

I think of the woman who swooped in and plastered herself all over him earlier.

Ryan could do better—not that he's looking for a serious relationship or given me an indication he is, but that's my hot take as someone who makes a living not just pouring drinks but listening to people.

"What about skating?" Nova suggests. "Trista said there was a pond here. Maybe if there is, there are skates around somewhere too."

We follow the directions she left us to the rink. We start down the path, and it's not long before we break through a stand of trees.

"Look!" Nova cries, delighted.

The little pond is iced over. It's pristine and pretty, and even I can't deny its charm.

Nova trips out onto the surface, slipping and laughing with glee. Brooke follows, running and sliding until she collides with her friend, grabbing her hands. They both go down in a giggling pile.

Jay's next, his sister demanding he help her up. Soon everyone's out there, running and sliding.

Not everyone's on the ice. I glance over to

see Ryan leaning against a tree, hands stuffed in his pockets and a serious expression on his face.

Okay, so I'm the Christmas grinch. I shouldn't kick a puppy when he's down, but I can't help it.

I sidle up to him. "Guess the tree wasn't meant to be."

"Oh, we're getting a tree." His gaze locks with mine, and I see he's determined, not sad. "No way that's getting in the way of the perfect Christmas."

Surprise has me snorting. "You're that worried about losing and having to do media?"

"Reporters are out for blood come January."

"What's the worst that could happen?"

He lifts a brow. "We're world champions. I say something stupid, next thing you know, it's all over social media. Every sports program in the world."

"That is pretty bad," I concede. "But you can't know exactly what sportscasters are going to say, so you'll do better if you just roll with it."

He folds his arms. His gaze flicks down me and back up. "Roll with it, huh?"

I'm suspicious but too late. He grabs my hands and tugs me toward the ice where the rest of the crew is laughing and shouting as they run and slide on the slick surface.

"Me and ice are not a good combination," I warn, digging in my heels.

It's as if I didn't put up any resistance at all. He's still tugging, and I'm tripping as he steps onto the ice first.

"You were the one who said we had to roll with it," he reminds me. He slides backward, graceful even without skates.

"*You.* You have to roll with it." My voice lifts at the end. I size up the slippery surface, wishing I'd worn grippier boots.

"Ahh. And you get to stay stuck in your ways?"

My foot makes contact with the ice, and I slide into him, grabbing at him to avoid falling.

I find his forearms, my fingers digging into corded muscle. "We're not talking about me," I grit out.

"You're good at listening to everyone else's problems," Ryan murmurs. "Who listens to you, bartender?"

His eyes lock with mine. Awareness starts in my chest, sends tingles that ripple outward.

"LOOK OUT!"

A mass of limbs collides with me in the form of Nova and Brooke. We collapse in a pile of mittens and earmuffs and combat boots, and I'm saved having to answer.

AFTER SOME TIME on the ice, Ryan's spirits are high once again.

"Dinner?" Atlas comments.

"You're always hungry," Jay counters.

"Course I am. How else you think I stay big enough to block the guys who come at you, huh?" He beats his chest.

We trudge through the woods back toward the cabin.

"All I'm saying is I was promised a feast."

"And a feast you'll have, big guy," Ryan proclaims. He's still wearing his Santa hat. "But satisfy yourself on my epic hot chocolate first. Anyone says it's not the best they've ever had, I'll fight them."

He's being completely ridiculous, but I can't resist smiling.

The forest is actually beautiful and quiet in a way the city never is. Snow feathers across branches and drifts lazily when the wind picks up. The sun sets and we pause to watch it.

"That's really pretty. Better than the view from our place," Nova says.

"Sounds like a vote for the perfect Christmas," Ryan starts.

Clay holds up a hand. "Not yet."

Brooke looks between them. "What's the big deal? You can't admit he did something right?"

"First, he's not responsible for the setting sun, no matter how much he'd like you to think so. Second—" Jay spins around. "What's that sound?"

We all go quiet.

It's Chloe who speaks next. "I didn't hear—"

This time there's a crack.

"It was a mile away at least," Jay decides. "It's quiet up here, so everything sounds closer."

"It was closer than that." Atlas cranes his neck to look. Being the closest to the sky, he probably has the best chance of catching sight of anything.

"Let's go back and make dinner," Ryan says.

We all head back to the cabin and shed our snowy layers. Miles lunges for the fireplace, getting the flames going in record time. Ryan makes hot chocolate, and I run point on cocktails.

Mile High is the watering hole for the team and its fans, only a few blocks from the stadium. My dad opened it more than two decades ago. I've worked there since I was old enough and practiced long before that.

I started by building an encyclopedic knowledge of drinks, but the people have always fascinated me as much as the cocktails. The margarita was probably invented by a woman. The mojito was originally medicinal. The negroni supposedly came to be when a count wanted his Americano stiffer, so he added gin instead of soda water.

Drinks are so much more than thirst quenchers. They bring people together. They tell our stories.

"Oooh, that looks fantastic," Nova observes.

I make her a drink and slide it over. Brooke takes a sip.

"Too much booze?" I ask.

"Maybe we can do no booze?" Nova requests. "I've been sleeping like crap lately working on this art show."

"You got it." I make her one without.

My dad always loves giving people what they ask for—usually beer—but I get a thrill out of coming up with new combinations. He's a traditionalist. That applies to what we serve but also how the bar operates. A lot of things he hasn't changed in twenty years.

As I keep reminding him, we're overdue, but he doesn't listen.

The entire crew eats around a big table. Nova suggests she and Clay take first shift cleaning up since Clay picked the first room. Clay's not sure about her logic, but she shoots him a look and he promptly follows her to the kitchen to wash dishes.

"We're having a holiday movie fest. Let's vote on it," Ryan decides.

The crew argues their cases for *The Santa Clause, Elf,* and *Home Alone.*

They land on *Elf.* The movie starts, and I

resist the tug of being charmed watching Buddy eat candy, make friends, and essentially try to find his home away from the North Pole in the most adorably cringe-inducing ways.

We're sitting around on couches and chairs, a few of us on the floor. Ryan's at the opposite end of the couch from me. Once in a while our feet brush.

Tingles in my stomach have me glancing over to find Ryan watching me. He cocks his head, lips curved.

"All good?" he mouths.

I nod quickly and look back at the TV... except the words are in my brain long after I retrain my eyes on the movie.

So is the feeling of Ryan's attention on me.

It's one thing to ignore how hot he is when we're in a busy bar and his picture is hanging on the wall of my family business. It's another to do it up here, in the secluded woods, where he's close and personal.

An hour into the movie, I duck back into the kitchen on the pretense of refilling drinks and use that opportunity to hit a contact on my phone.

"Hey, kid," Dad answers. "Did you make my favorite drinks?"

"How'd you know?"

He laughs. "I know everything about you."

Not everything. I want to say it even though it's childish.

"Don't forget, the new stools are coming tomorrow," I remind him.

"Tell me you didn't order those." I can practically hear him grimace.

"They were on sale. We've needed them for months. The old ones have holes." My voice is firm.

"So, we'll patch them up. I'll return these."

"Dad..." I groan, rubbing a hand over my face.

New stools barely scratch the surface of what I'd do if Mile High were my bar, but Dad's beyond resistant to anything I try to bring in, from new menu offerings and suppliers to décor. Even so, fighting me on replacing seating that saw its best days twenty years ago is ridiculous.

"They don't come here for change, honey. They don't want fancy stools. They want cold beer, the team winning, a place that feels like it's theirs. It's not about me, and it's not about you."

It's not about you.

The reminder is kind of heartbreaking. I give my all to that place yet still feel as though I can't make a difference beyond selling more beers. I can't put my fingerprint on Mile High because it's all about the team.

"Too much phone time for the holidays." Clay's over my shoulder as I hang up.

"So, Ryan's the Christmas King and you're the phone police?" I tease him.

The Kodiaks' five-time all-star is intimidating to most people, but we've had him over for family dinner more than once.

"Something like that. Your dad?"

"Sure was."

"How's the bar?"

"It's up and down."

He opens his mouth, and I know it's to offer help, so I lift a hand before he can say the words.

"You've done more than enough. As Dad always says, the Kodiaks winning is the best advertisement." I send him a smile and head back out to the living room.

Ryan

SURPRISINGLY, the girls tap out first. Our day is drawing to a close, and they've been talking a good game, but Chloe waves the flag.

"I've been busy keeping your asses out of trouble." She points a finger around the group, then hides a yawn with her hand.

"We're angels, Chlo," Jay protests from the lounge chair. He's rewarded with a dirty look.

My gaze lands on Sierra. It's been drifting to her for hours, every time my attention wanders. She's curled up in a beanbag chair as if she's leaving the couch for the couples.

More than that, she's preoccupied.

We've been up watching movies all night. Once in a while, we've checked in on the LA game, but the girls wouldn't let us leave the TV there, saying it's a holiday and there's no basketball allowed.

I wonder what she's thinking about.

"It is probably time," Nova agrees, yawning.

Fuck. The sleepiness is contagious.

Clay's hand threads through hers. No one in the entire NBA can bring our all-star to his knees faster than his pink-haired pixie of a wife.

I'm still humming with energy. We have to get the most out of our time here. "Come on, guys. The night is young. We can watch another one. Atlas?"

Our big man is an easy yes when it comes to group activities. He's always down for an extra drink or social event.

"I'm going to call some family back home. It's morning over there." He rises and pads toward the stairs.

"Jay?"

"Nah."

Miles and Brooke head upstairs.

I ignore them and wait a beat before pressing. "Sierra?"

If there's a reasonable amount of hope for one guy to have about a woman saying she'll hang out with him, I've exceeded it.

"I'd better not," she says at last. She's standing too.

Disappointment crashes over me. It's like losing a close game at the buzzer.

I hear Jay and Brooke talking upstairs about some Christmas when they were kids.

And then I'm alone.

The cabin is quiet. Creaky.

I fix another drink and return to the fire.

I think about my family back in Kentucky —the things we'd do for the holidays, the line of stockings along the fireplace. I drag a finger along the mantel.

Then I switch off the lights and head upstairs too.

5

RYAN

There's a bear in here. One that's rumbling and roaring.

I jolt awake, sitting straight up in bed. The bear rumbles again from my right.

It's only Jay snoring under the covers of his bunk.

"He didn't used to be this loud," I mutter, astounded. We've been on the road to games, sleeping on planes, and I can't remember this noise.

"He was worse." Atlas's voice comes from the top bunk.

I shake my head and get up. There are sounds downstairs, and when I stick my head out of the room, I smell coffee brewing.

My stomach growls louder than Jay in his sleep.

When I step into the bathroom, my hair is sticking up all over the place. Guess I didn't sleep the best—probably due to the bunk bed situation. What seemed cozy in theory is a little rough in practice. I'm used to a king bed, and anything less means I've got body parts hanging off the sides.

But it's not nearly as rough as the time we went camping as kids and my sister dropped her sleeping blanket in the lake so I gave her mine. I thought I'd never know how it felt to be warm again, though I wouldn't have complained out loud. The chill only lasted a few hours, and the smile on her face made up for it.

Funny how quick you get used to the way things are.

Now, I grab a quick shower and tug on purple plaid Kodiaks pants.

There's no early-morning workout or game tape watching session. For two days, we're free and we're together.

I get down to the kitchen, expecting to find Miles already working his barista magic. The guy can brew a mean espresso and do it for a crowd.

"Miles. My favorite guard..." I start, leaning over the island that separates the dining area from the kitchen.

It's not Miles.

Sierra's standing next to the coffee machine, her hair tucked up in two little buns on her head. A soft purple tank top, the same shade as her shorts, reveals fascinating tattoos. She's drumming her fingers on the countertop as the coffee brews.

Hell yes.

There's no part of this I'm not instantly committing to memory.

"Morning," I say at last.

Sierra opens a pine cabinet over the sink. "Ran out of clothes on day one?" she asks as she pulls four mugs off the first shelf. "You *could* put a shirt on."

"But I get such a great reception when I don't."

Now she does look at me, toes to tips. I lean over the island, flexing for her benefit.

I hitch a thumb upstairs. "If it's bothering you, I can—"

"I'm not affected."

"Right."

She seems affected. She turns away again and presses up onto her toes, trying to reach more mugs at the top. I round the island to her, nudging her out of the way with a hip.

"My grandfather swears he won my grandmother over with his *cafecito*." I reach the mugs easily and pass them to her.

"He makes it strong?"

I grin. "He'd say, *Esto te despierta hasta las ideas.* It'll even wake up your brain cells."

She laughs as she sets the mugs on the counter in tidy rows.

Although he came to Tampa and married my grandmother fifty years ago, he still loves to share his food, stories, and music at every opportunity.

"I hope you weren't up too late drinking alone last night."

I file away the fact that she noticed. "I wasn't drinking alone. I was thinking about home."

She turns that over as the coffee machine beeps. "What about it?"

"On Christmas day, we'd go outside and look for reindeer tracks in the snow."

"Did you find them?"

"Never." I go to the fridge, pulling out cream as she gets sugar from a drawer. "My parents tried to convince us the cat's footprints were reindeer though. I said the reindeer work in a team, so there weren't enough tracks."

"Smart kid. When did you catch on?"

"I was seven or eight. But once I was in high school, I took over making it work for my cousins."

"Cute."

"How about you? What's your best Christmas memory?"

She turns the question over before answering. "One year there was a huge storm. Dad couldn't get to the bar, so it was closed. I got a chemistry set and played with it the entire holiday and made him play with me." Her lips curve at the memory.

I grew up with a big family, and they were a massive part of my life. Taking care of each other was just how we rolled. Her family was smaller, and taking care of each other was a necessity.

"You worry about him."

"Running the bar has been hard work for a long time, and he thinks he has to do it alone. I wish he'd see that I'm here. Except…" She blows out a breath. "I don't want to do things like he does. I have my own ideas. And I think I've earned the space to try them out."

"So, why don't you?"

Sierra shoots me a look. "Because he reminds me that's not how we do things. But what he means is, it's not how he does things. Sometimes it feels like it would be easier if I worked somewhere else."

It's obvious how much she cares about her family and feels responsible for their business.

"You ever tell him that?"

"No." She laughs. "It's not going to happen."

"You can practice on me, if you want."

She looks up, our eyes locking. "I'm not afraid."

It feels so damn good to stand close to her. I'm wondering what she'd do if I backed her against the counter. Lifted her onto it, my fingers digging into her curvy hips.

A loud noise like a grunt comes from outside the window.

She jumps, spilling half the contents of her mug on the floor and herself, plus a few drops on me. "What the hell was that?"

Not that I care about the spillage, because she's tucked against my side. I tuck her closer behind me and peer outside.

Her hand is on my bare chest, her breasts pressing against me through her tank top. When her chin lifts, her gaze meeting mine, I'm aware of all the places we're lined up.

I'm thrown back to this time last year—the hookup no one since has measured up to.

Probably because what I feel about her isn't only physical. This woman who's cool and confident and sexy, with layers behind the walls she keeps high to keep people out... All of it only made me want more badly to break inside.

The front door has us jumping apart.

"A storm is coming!" Chloe announces. She shoves the hood of her parka off her face and stomps snow off her boots onto the rug.

"You go for a hike?" I ask.

"More like a wade. It's so deep. I went up to

the road but no cars." She shrugs out of the coat and adjusts her ponytail. "Coffee? Oh God, yes."

Sierra's already passing over a mug.

As if called by ESP, Brooke sticks her head out of her doorway at the top of the stairs. Miles is next.

Soon, the table is half occupied.

"I think I'm going to go for a run today," Brooke volunteers as she claims a seat on the far side with Chloe.

"Good luck with that," I say.

"Don't go alone," Sierra says from the kitchen as I take the head of the table. "We heard noises outside."

"What kind of noises?" Brooke asks.

Sierra cocks her head. "It was probably Trista trying to score a look at Ryan naked."

I snort.

The crew talks for a few minutes as I take a sip of my coffee. Damn, that's good.

"I have some gift wrapping to do," Nova volunteers, presumably for our secret Santa exchange later on. "Clay's going to help me."

"I'd pay money to have Clayton Wade wrap my gifts."

"You couldn't afford me." Clay's voice comes from the stairs, where he's shuffling down them one at a time. He might play the old man, but he's one of the most legendary players ever. Like Kobe or LeBron. Like them, he can say as much with a look as with a word.

Sierra's gone back to the kitchen. That won't do.

"We also need to get the tree," I say as I shift out of my seat, my mug still in my hand.

I head for the kitchen, draining the rest of my mug on the way. The caffeine kicks pleasantly in my veins, the warm flavor dancing on my tongue.

I find Sierra bent over inside the open fridge. Her curvy ass is hugged by her shorts, her long legs pale and ending in bunny slippers.

"You hiding out here?"

She emerges with two cartons of eggs and some bacon balanced on top. "Starting breakfast."

"Easy, Cirque du Soleil." I reach for the bacon as it slides off.

"Thanks," she murmurs when I grab it, one-handed, before it hits the floor.

"You know, for someone who practically lives with the team, you act like we bite sometimes."

"Well, bears and humans aren't a good combination," she says under her breath. I don't have time to press her on that because she continues, "Besides, I enjoy cooking."

She kicks the fridge closed with a bunny foot and sets the eggs on the counter. Under the sink, she rummages around until she finds a big frying pan.

I set my mug on the counter. "Bet you're good at it too. But how often do you let someone else do the heavy lifting?"

She puts the pan on the stove, turns on the element, and cuts a chunk of butter into it. "If I waited, I'd be waiting a long time. I'm not a famous athlete with thousands of fans ready to worship me."

"I don't believe that for a second. You've got more than a few worshippers at Mile High."

Her lips twitch. "They like me because I pour the alcohol."

"They like you because you're funny. And kind. And..."

"What?" She leans a hip against the

counter, face tilted up reluctantly. Her lips are parted, her dark eyes alert and warm.

I pause. "And way too fucking beautiful."

Sierra turns away and grabs a couple of eggs, but not before I see her flush. "Save it for the Kodashians, Ryan. You don't need to pretend what happened last year was a big deal. We're cool."

I frown as she taps an egg on the edge of the pan, cracking it in.

"We are?" I ask slowly.

Sierra turns for a handful more, but I'm right there to pass eggs to her. She jumps, taking them from me. Our fingers brush. Our eyes lock.

"Yeah. It was a one-time thing. Meaningless."

My appetite evaporates in an instant.

I didn't realize how much it would suck to hear her say those words. Not like I'm head over heels, but I think about her a lot. About last year, what was and what might have been. Now, if there was any hope left alive that she was into it, that hope is dying an agonizing death.

Once she's done, she dodges me and goes to the sink to wash her hands.

Then she wipes down the counter thoroughly. Carefully.

"You take almost as good care of this as your bar at home," Brooke observes from the other room.

"You've got no idea," Clay counters. "Her bar is sacred. It's her altar."

That's when it clicks.

I step closer to her. "How many times have you hooked up on your bar, Sierra?"

Her eyes flicker.

Laughter goes up from the dining room. Neither of us looks over.

"Let me guess: one-time thing, meaningless," I say quietly. A slow smile tugs at my lips.

I whistle—Mariah Carey—as I go in search of the toaster.

I'm suddenly starving again.

6

CLAY

A guy with two world championships and more all-star appearances than anyone deserves to have should be unmovable. A rock. A fortress.

But when Nova says, "Strip," I do it faster than I can get off a shot from the elbow.

"How's the knee?" she asks.

"I'm thirty-five, not seventy," I grunt.

My wife lifts a brow but otherwise doesn't acknowledge my protest.

Our room is compact but surprisingly comfortable. There's a woodstove on one wall, a rug on the floor, and most importantly, a bed big enough for both of us.

Sure, I take up three quarters of it.

I sit on the edge of the bed, the mattress creaking under me, and drag up one pant leg. "I was looking forward to a couple days without the training staff."

Nova prods my knee with her fingers. She's not a physio, but she's learned as much about it and my injury as she can since we've been together.

My wife's an artist, first, last, always. Since we met, I've been drawn to the way she sees the world, back when she was running away from her past and finding her future. Her art has always given her a way to look at other people and life.

I hope I'm every bit as supportive of her as she is of me.

"You're cleared for duty," she decides, straightening.

At her full height, with me seated, our faces are level.

Convenient.

"Good. I'm ready to give you exactly what you need." I grab her waist and drag her into my lap.

There's no time I'm not interested in getting my wife naked. It's one thing to focus on the court when we have a game to play, but we're officially off duty until tomorrow. No number of teammates or dinners or planned fun would beat time with Nova.

Preferably naked.

Her pink hair splayed over my tattoos…

"Not that kind of duty! Get your boots."

My fantasy evaporates. "Thought we were wrapping presents?"

"We are."

I follow her downstairs, and we dress in our outdoor stuff. I hold the door, and we step outside into the snow.

"It's so beautiful here!" she calls, clutching the basket she found in the kitchen.

"What're we looking for?"

"Anything pretty that's fallen off the trees." Nova paces toward the edge of the forest, bends, and triumphantly holds up a pinecone.

"You're the expert in artistic things."

"Nice try. You're not getting out of it, Clay."

"How's this?" I ask, deadpan.

"That looks like animal poop."

"So that's a no."

She shakes her head.

I find a sprig of berries. "Better?"

Her eyes light up. "That's perfect!" She takes it and twirls it in her fuzzy purple mittens. "Nothing's touched them. Inside are the next generation of bushes and trees. It's amazing what nature can produce."

She sighs as she drops the stick of berries into her basket. I sense her mood shift to thoughtful as if it's happening inside me.

Before her, all I could think about was my life, my career, my legacy. Ask any sports journalist and I'm among the best who ever played.

But they don't talk about you after you stop setting foot on that court.

Sure, you can buy a team, take on a GM role, find a way to steal a corner of the spotlight or stay in the league.

I'm nearing retirement and have decided that's not what I want. I'm not about to trade a long-ass work week in a jersey for the same one in a suit.

I glance at the gray sky as snow falls.

Nova and I got married a year ago, and we've been working on our own project.

She wants kids. I wasn't sure I did, not before her. Now, I feel as though I have something to contribute.

We've been trying for a few months, and it hasn't happened yet. Still, as much as it would be a rush to know that she's pregnant, she's enough for me exactly the way she is.

"You good, Pink?" I step closer, nudging her small boots with my big ones.

"Yeah." She peers into her basket, assessing. "What's happening with Ryan and Sierra?"

"What do you mean?"

She nods toward the cabin. "He has a thing for her. Does he give off any signals?"

I shake my head. "I dunno, Pink. We run up and down a court. I don't ask him about his star sign or who he has a crush on."

"Maybe the team would be even closer if you did."

"We're plenty close. He's my rookie and we won a championship together." I laugh, plucking the basket from her hands. "Besides, you're so tight with the bartender, how come you don't know?"

Nova shoots me a look before continuing along the treeline, inspecting the ground for anything else that inspires her. "She hasn't dated anyone that I know of. She's always working. And probably tired of getting hit on."

"Wait. So, you think *my* rookie isn't good enough for her?" I'm not offended, but I am ready to defend my teammate.

Nova laughs, a tinkling music that lights me up. "Jury's still out."

There's a knocking sound behind us. I swivel and inspect the treeline.

"What's that?" Nova asks.

I pause. "Maybe whatever crapped in the woods."

"Are there bears around here?"

"Mhmm. Kodiaks. Better look out." I growl and drop the basket so I can scoop her up.

She squeals. "You promised you'd protect me," she gasps between laughing, out of breath when I set her down.

"Today. Tomorrow. Every day I get."

She bends to collect her basket. When she straightens, her lips curve. I tip her chin up toward me.

The knocking sound comes again, and we both jump.

"But just in case, let's go inside," she says.

Nova

"You were gone a long time," Chloe calls when we head back inside with my basket of decorations. "Get any pine needles in your back from banging in the trees?"

She's sitting at the kitchen table opposite Brooke.

"The only pine needles are for wrapping," I offer.

"Did you see Miles while you were out there?" Brooke asks me. "I seem to have misplaced my fiancé."

I frown, shaking my head.

"Maybe Trista kidnapped him," Jay suggests, looking up from his phone.

"Maybe Ryan's with him and Trista kidnapped both of them," Chloe finishes.

Jay scoffs. "You could sound more concerned as the head of PR for the team."

"Long as they're back home in time to get ready for the game, I'm happy."

"So, you wouldn't care if she kidnapped me? What if I disappeared? Would you come rescue me?"

Chloe flicks her gaze up and down Jay.

"Possibly. You're our point guard, and we don't have a good backup." She turns to her phone. "The storm is getting closer."

Jay whistles. "Maybe we'll get stuck here tomorrow."

"Don't even joke about that. We have to be back in time for the Christmas game."

Clay shifts next to me, and suddenly I'm more aware of him than anyone else in the room.

I feel my hair move and glance over to see him flicking my ponytail. "You had snow there."

Once in a while, it still hits me that I'm married to one of the most famous players in the entire league. He's a legend.

And he's all mine.

"You cold?" he asks.

Clay's looking down at me, and suddenly I'm warm everywhere.

"No. I mean, yes."

His eyes spark too, and he takes the basket from me. "C'mon."

"Where are you guys going?"

"Wrapping presents!" I call.

Which we do have to do, but also, he's

looking at me in that way that still sets me on fire long after the first time he did it.

Inside our room, he shuts the door.

I spread paper, scissors, and tape out on the bed next to the basket of items and kneel on the rug facing the bed. I fish some precut ribbons and bows from my bag next to me. "I think I'll do different patterns for each gift."

Clay takes a pink ribbon in one hand and gently captures my wrist with the other.

"I found something to wrap." He ties the ribbon lightly around my wrist.

"You missed one."

His eyes warm, but instead of doing the same to my other wrist, he holds them together and ties another ribbon around both of them. His eyes meet mine, and I'm torn between getting this wrapping done and tapping out.

What are you supposed to do when the hottest player in the game is looking at you like you're all he wants to unwrap?

"I figured between all the trying we've been doing, you'd be tired," I whisper.

He barks out a laugh. "I'm not dead."

My lips curve too. He's a serious guy, so any time I can make him smile is a win for me.

"Besides, think I need to get a good look at what I'm wrapping."

He lifts and turns me so I'm sitting on the edge of the bed, my feet brushing the rug. The wrapping supplies are scattered around me. Next, he's reaching for the hem of my shirt and tugging it up over my body. I'm only in my bra.

My shirt won't come off my tied wrists. He leans over me and follows me down when my shoulders hit the bed. His lips skim along my collarbone, down over my breasts. His mouth sucks on one side until I'm writhing.

"You've abandoned the wrapping project," I protest.

"I'm doing it my own way."

He tugs my leggings down over my hips, dragging my thong with them. I'm bare, and he takes me in as though I'm everything he wants —for Christmas and all the days between.

Clay's fingers brush between my thighs. I arch against him.

He reaches for a little branch of pine needles.

"What are you going to do with…?"

He drags it down my slit, and my eyes close. My wrists strain against the ribbon. He presses them to the bed. I'm already gasping when his mouth descends between my legs.

I want everything with this man. The world doesn't know him like I do, doesn't get him like I do.

And after all we've been through, we still have a lifetime ahead of us.

"You know my favorite Christmas?" he asks.

I shake my head.

"Any one with you in it."

7

———

SIERRA

"You get any?" Chloe asks when she comes into the living room where I'm on the couch reading a magazine.

I blink and look up. "Any what?"

"Reception."

It's the afternoon, and we're hanging out in the living room. Even I have to admit it's a little relaxing.

"You want to borrow my phone?" I ask.

"It's okay. I'm trying to keep tabs on this storm. We have to be back tomorrow morning."

Her gaze falls to my magazine.

"You ever been to South Beach?" Chloe asks. The glossy pages are a travel special about Miami—the sights, the bars and restaurants.

I shake my head. "I haven't had a lot of chances to travel. Running the bar with my dad, I can't exactly take off." I flip a page, wondering what that would feel like.

"I get what it's like trying to make your own way. When I joined the Kodiaks, there was a lot of cleanup to do."

I glance at Chloe. She's always struck me as hyper-capable and confident. "You could work anywhere. Why do you stay?"

She claims a stool next to the island. "It's the guys. They're like family. You know how it is."

I'm still processing that as Jay descends the stairs, holding up his phone. "LA wants to hand us our asses tomorrow."

"Clay seen this trash talk?" Atlas asks. "We should show him—"

"Pretty sure you won't come back out with eyes."

"Guys. We'll have plenty of time to come back at them when we're well rested and fed tomorrow," Chloe says.

"New rule: no phones." Ryan grabs Jay's

phone out of his hand.

"Dude, you're out of line."

The phone slips, making a sickening cracking sound as it hits the floor.

"Shit."

"Dammit, Ryan!" Jay retrieves his phone, holding it up to reveal a big crack in the screen.

"This can't be the perfect Christmas without a tree." Ryan stomps toward the door. "I'm going to get a saw."

"Get me a new phone while you're at it?!" Jay calls.

The door slams shut.

The guys in the cabin go back to arguing, but I shove myself off the couch and chase after Ryan. My boots slip in the snow as I run out into the snowy afternoon.

"You can't cut down a tree solo," I call after I yank on my coat.

"Watch me." Ryan trudges to the shed.

I tromp through the snow after him. Is it deeper than the last time I was out? If not, it will be soon.

"What was that about?" I ask as I catch up.

"Nothing," he grunts, but his shoulders are

hunched as though he's in a bad mood about Jay.

Ryan ignores the lock and wedges his fingers into the opening.

"Still no luck with a key," I deduce.

He shakes his head. "Trista offered to come and replace the lock. Figured I'd save us some time." With a few hard yanks, the screws holding the lock give way and the shed door opens.

It's kind of sexy, this lumberjack version of him, though I'm not about to admit it.

Inside, the shed is packet with outdoor toys and tools.

"I thought that coming to this cabin would help everyone bond and take a weight off, stop thinking about the game and everything going on," Ryan says as he rummages through a work bench.

"It is," I insist. "Everyone is having a good time."

He doesn't answer. When he turns up a saw, he nods in satisfaction.

We walk through the woods together, me rushing to keep pace with him. He doesn't notice, his breath puffing in the cold and his hair curling against his forehead.

"Tell me more about your normal Christmas. What's it like if you're not with the team?" I ask.

"Lots of meals. My mom taught me to cook."

"So you kids could fend for yourselves?"

"More like she didn't want us winding up being a burden on our partners."

I'm surprised, but maybe I shouldn't be. "That's very cool of her."

"She's a cool lady."

I snort.

"What?"

"You just described your mom as a cool lady."

"She is." He cuts me a curious look, grinning. "So, why are you such a grinch?"

I don't want to get into it, but Ryan's so charming and roguish, and being here with him in the snow makes it feel as though everything is easy.

"Growing up with a family sports bar, Christmas was just another day. We worked.

Instead of opening presents in pajamas, we were refilling drinks and running food."

"No traditions?"

"Not really. Another day with better tips."

"I'm sorry."

I look up to see him watching me, his dark brows pulled together. I force a laugh. "Don't be. It's the job."

He's being so sweet. In my line of work, I hear a lot of people talk about their problems. Maybe not as many as some bartenders because it's a fast-paced sports bar and not some backstreet dive, but I care about other people and can tell when another person's interest is genuine.

It sounds as if Ryan actually cares about me and my life.

I lick my lips. "So, what kind of tree are we looking for?"

"The perfect fit for the cabin."

"A small one."

"Nope, there's that peaked roof. Right over by the woodstove is the perfect spot. It's got to be twelve feet tall at least."

He would know, as he's a lot closer to that height than I am.

"How about that one?" I point at a modest-looking tree.

"I was thinking more like that." He nods toward a massive one, and I laugh out loud.

"Small problem—we have to get it back there."

"Easy peasy." He drops the saw into the snow and plants his hands on his hips. "I work out."

"Obviously." I meant because he's a pro athlete and that's part of the job, but a memory's coming back to me. Maybe it's coming back to him too, because his eyes heat.

I'm thinking back to that kitchen, when he called me out.

"How many times have you hooked up on your bar, Sierra?"

Sensations flash through my body, memories that I'm suddenly reliving.

I shake off the haze.

"Christmas wasn't all bad," I hear myself say. "Mile High is always open on Christmas Day, especially if there's a Kodiaks game. I'm an only child, so we didn't have big gatherings. But when I was old enough to be a fan, my dad always gave me something from the team. He tried to find something unique. Even if it wasn't expensive, he wanted it to be special."

"The team means a lot to you."

I feel a smile tug at my lips. "The bar gave my dad a way to plug into his favorite passion. I guess he passed that on to me. It's probably stupid, building your whole life around a team."

"Not at all. It's people. And pride. And a purpose."

I turn that over. "I'm surprised you're so sentimental."

He shrugs. "Holidays aren't about buying shit. They're a vessel for whatever you want to pour into them."

When Ryan speaks, it's as though he's thought about it. That alone impresses me, but coupled with what he's saying... there's so much more to this guy than I gave him credit for.

I look past him. "How about that one?"

We cross to the tree, and he inspects it. "Perfect," he decides.

He drops a rope he brought with him on the ground and takes up his position.

"You ever done his before, Christmas King?" I ask, folding my arms.

"Nope. But I'm a fast learner." He starts to saw.

Five minutes later, he strips off his coat and passes it to me.

"Ready to tap out?" I ask as I take it.

"Just warming up." But he swipes a hand over his brow.

He's glistening in the sun. Not like *Twilight* vampire glistening, just a bead of sweat on his forehead.

I want to lick it off.

Ryan is hot. I've seen him on TV, even spent enough time with him in person that I could draw him from memory.

At least, if my art skills were more like Nova's and less like a five-year-old's attempt at their first stick person.

Point is, I've never had the chance to just watch him up close.

His body moves effortlessly, his muscles bulging under the shirt. His brows pull together in concentration, his lips parted as he works.

Awareness prickles low in my stomach.

I'm imagining him focused on me instead of that tree. There's a sweet ache low in my stomach. I can't remember when it started, but it's growing every minute.

"Get ready," he says.

I blink. "For what?" My voice is rough.

"The tree's going to fall that way." He points my direction.

It does, but a little more angled than I expected.

"Ryan…" my voice rises at the end.

I'm paralyzed. I can't move.

Fucking move.

He dives for me and knocks me out of the way. I hit the ground hard. Or at least I would if there weren't a foot of snow on everything.

The sun burns the backs of my eyelids. *Breathe.*

"Sierra." Ryan's urgent voice comes from above me.

Close.

I nod because I can't speak.

It's agonizingly long before I manage to suck in air. "Just got the wind knocked out of me."

I crack open my eyes to see him over me.

He's straddling me, his weight on his hands and knees.

"It was worth it to have perfect Christmas decoration," I pant.

Ryan laughs, and it feels every bit as good as anything I can remember. "I forgot mistletoe," he admits.

I snort. "My first kiss ever was under the mistletoe at a Christmas party."

"Ahh. And it was so bad you've hated the holidays ever since."

"No!" I laugh. "I was ten. I had a huge crush on this guy, Dustin."

"And he laid one on you?"

"I kissed him."

"I like a woman who knows what she wants."

Snow sneaks in under the back of my jacket, getting on my skin and ripping me from my thoughts with a shocking cold. I screech an embarrassingly high-pitched sound.

Ryan immediately sizes up what's happening and rolls me so I'm on top. "Better?"

I'm over him, my mittens braced under his arms because he's too tall for me to reach above his shoulders. Every part of us is touching.

Damn, he's huge. I've seen him like this before, but it's different now.

"Ryan…"

A clump of snow hits the back of my head.

He chuckles. The vibration has me feeling the warmth of him through our clothes.

"How come you're on the bottom and the snow still got me?" I demand as I brush at my hair.

"I'm the Christmas King." His grins widens.

But I'm smiling too.

My jacket is undone, and his is on the ground a few feet away. I've never been so aware of what I'm wearing, and not wearing.

"That kiss with Dustin," he says after a minute, "if you want to reenact it, I'm your guy."

Breathing is hard. It has nothing to do with the fact that his weight was crushing me a few moments ago.

"There's no mistletoe. Besides…" I swallow. "Kissing you is different."

A bird chirps in the forest, flying overhead.

Ryan's eyes darken. "I figured you'd forgotten, seeing as how you never mentioned it again."

"That's not true."

"What, that you forgot or haven't mentioned it?"

His hands are still on my hips.

"I—either. Both?"

At my bar, I'm the one in control. Here, between the holiday cheer and the great outdoors and the fact that I watched the hottest man I've ever seen cut down a tree, I'm so out of my element.

His attention drops to my mouth. I shift over him, suddenly unable to keep still.

"You're making this harder," I complain.

"What?" He props himself up on his elbows and brings us closer. His eyes are inches away and so beautiful it's unfair.

"Resisting you."

Triumph flashes across his handsome face.

Ryan's thumbs dig into my hips. "I'm sorry."

I search his eyes. "No, you're not."

"No, I'm not," he whispers.

Then he closes the distance between us.

8

SIERRA

The moment he's kissing me, I'm sinking into him.

His lips are firm and warm. His tongue is a tease that makes me want to open and go deeper at once.

It's even hotter than I remember, which is a pretty high bar.

I shift over him, moaning as I feel the friction of his body between my thighs.

I kiss him back. It feels so good. No responsibilities, no rules, no tomorrow.

Ryan groans triumphantly into my mouth. Then he grabs the back of my head and drags me closer. His other hand finds my thigh, digging into my skin.

Yes, I could get behind this kind of Christmas.

He grips my hips, encouraging me to grind over him.

We're both getting friction burns if this keeps up. If it's possible to give fewer than zero fucks, I do.

My hands sneak beneath the hem of his shirt, and the feel of his smooth skin over the muscles of his abs almost makes me come right there.

"Your body is unreal," I mumble. "I didn't know it was possible to have this many abs."

He chuckles as his lips trail down my jaw, skimming just above the collar of my sweater.

"You feel pretty great yourself."

I wish I'd made the bold choice to wear a tank top in the snow today so he'd have better access.

I shouldn't have doubted him, because his hand slips to the inside of my thigh, his thumb rubbing me right where I ache.

Every muscle in me spasms at once.

I arch against his touch, chasing the feeling. "Yes, right there."

Damn, it's so good.

"Admit it," he murmurs against my mouth.

"What?" That shallow, pathetic excuse for a voice is definitely mine.

"You like me."

I sink my teeth into his lip. "You're not the worst."

His thumb stills between my thighs. His other hand, threaded in my hair, pulls me back an inch.

"What the hell?" I protest. I'm dazed from the change of sensation and the sunlight suddenly lighting up my retinas again.

Mostly what I care about as I settle my weight over his hard body—because, hello, he's hard *everywhere* now, and it's a serious distraction—is that we're not kissing.

Unless he's ready to dial this up another notch by using his mouth somewhere different, I do *not* approve of this development.

"Not the worst?" Ryan challenges, his eyelashes still at half-mast. But there's a stubbornness on his face that serves as a warning. "Come on. I enjoy your company, and you enjoy mine. Even if you try not to. It's not that hard to admit you're into me."

My mouth works. I'm still throbbing, first

from his touch and now from the absence of it. "It's not your company I'm appreciating most right now." I rock over him for emphasis, the first drag of friction sending pleasure dancing through me. When his teeth grind together, I'm triumphant.

"If it was only that, you would have forgotten about it by now. But you haven't. I'm willing to bet you can't stop thinking about me."

I still over him. "How exactly?"

His throat bobs, and he takes a breath. "Because I can't stop thinking about you."

We stare each other down for a long moment until a noise splits the forest.

"Marco?" a voice hollers.

"Polo!" another from the same direction hollers.

"*They're* supposed to say 'Polo.'"

The voices are getting closer. I start to shift off him, but he pulls me back to murmur in my ear. "If you think I'm going to let you pretend this didn't happen, you're out of your mind."

I trip off Ryan and shove myself to standing.

"You need any help getting that tree back?"

Miles and Atlas appear in the clearing just as I'm brushing the snow off my pants.

My cheeks are hot. I hope to hell I don't look as flushed as I feel.

"We'll take it," I answer for both of us.

9

———

SIERRA

LAST CHRISTMAS

"**S**hit. It's really coming down," Jenny calls from across the bar where she's wiping down tables by the door.

I cross to the nearest window and peer out, drying my hands on a towel. Huge flakes of snow cover the street outside. A couple of cars are parked under the streetlights, but there's no sign of their owners. If this weather continues, they might be stuck there.

"Go home," I decide.

"You don't need to close up alone," she protests.

"I've got this. You must have something to do for the holidays."

She sighs, her shoulders relaxing. "Wrapping for days, actually. Including something for this new guy I'm seeing."

I laugh as I go back behind the bar. "Sounds exciting."

"It is. It's new, and this is our first holiday together. But I guess that's how you make traditions, right? You don't know they're traditions until later." She goes to the back to collect her coat and purse, then heads for the door. "Sierra, are you—"

"Positive! We're closed. I'm nearly done. Have a good night. And Merry Christmas."

With a wave, she leaves.

Mariah Carey comes on, and I switch the playlist from holiday tunes to more bluesy tracks.

Most people are ready for the holiday. I have my shopping done. I'll swap gifts with some friends and family. There's no one I'm seeing.

Not that I'm lonely. I'm too busy for that.

I head to the back to grab more whisky, thinking of Ryan flirting with me. Letting myself enjoy the attention from someone I was attracted to felt good.

Then he kissed me.

One second, we were barely touching.

The next, he was surrounding me.

The move stole my breath. He was warm and so damn giving.

I wanted all of it. All of him.

My fingers fisted in his shirt, my feet clumsy as I tripped backward, him following easily.

"Sierra." His mouth started at my ear. A groan that traveled to my jaw, my throat, my collarbone.

"Yes."

It was supposed to be an answer to him saying my name.

It was an answer to something else.

Yes, you feel so good.

Yes, this is a terrible idea.

Yes, keep fucking going.

When we knocked the jar of cherries off the shelf, the glass banging on the floor and nearly shattering brought me back to reality.

Ryan tried to stick around, but I shoved him out the door faster than you could say "holiday hookup."

When I made it back out to the bar, I

managed to avoid him for the better part of an hour until one time I looked up and he was gone.

It was over. A thrilling, if embarrassing, slipup that I will absolutely replay one night with my hand between my thighs when I'm horny and have zero shame.

Now, I'm tired. Maybe I'm coming down with something. I press a hand to my forehead. Not hot. Need to sleep more.

I finish wiping down the tables Jenny didn't get to, my hips swaying to the music. Then I return to the bar, taking my time.

I play around with a few cocktails. There's nothing I need to be home for. I take out the cherries, wanting to make something that's not so basic and cliché.

A few moments later, I have it. I take a sip. It's good but not quite right.

It needs a name.

Fifteen minutes later, I've made three new drinks. They're lined up in front of me, and I lean on the bar as I taste one after another.

Better.

Another sip of each to be sure.

A sound outside makes me jump. I didn't lock the door.

I trip a little as I round the bar. I guess I've had a couple of drinks, which sneaks up on you when you're taste-testing.

A man is on the other side of the door. I screech before recognizing his face and pulling the door open.

"Ryan?!"

His frame fills the doorway, snow covering his dark, curly hair. Shadows fall across his face. I step back to let him in, and he follows, stomping the snow off his shoes.

"I thought you left with those women." I reach past him to pull the door closed, locking it.

He's big and warm, and I'm suddenly aware of his presence and what almost went down in the back room.

He shakes his head. "I could've given them a cardboard cutout of me and they wouldn't have known the difference."

I laugh and head back to the bar. "What can I do for you?"

"Just wanted to let you know you might

have a hard time getting out of here, see if you need a ride."

His thoughtfulness is touching, but I'm not about to believe he left and then came all the way back to check on me.

I go back to the bar. "Is this you avoiding Christmas shopping?"

"Not at 3 a.m."

"Online," I offer.

"I guess."

"You don't need to buy for anyone special?"

"Do the guys count? Jay is a present snob and gets annoyed if you don't find him something great."

I laugh as he takes a seat on the stool where he was before, but now it's only the two of us. Ryan shrugs out of his coat.

My gaze lands on the bar. "Well, I don't need a rescue, but I could use an opinion." I slide a glass over to him.

He takes it, his gaze on mine as he sips. "That's incredible."

"Yeah?" I flush with pride.

"Why isn't it on the menu?"

"My dad wants to keep things traditional. Focus on the team."

"Fuck the team. Kidding," he goes on at my look. "But maybe you can honor the team and still do your own thing."

I reach under the bar for the good whisky and pull it out. His brows shoot up.

"Damn. Merry Christmas is right." He chuckles.

I pour us each one on the rocks and slide his over. We click glasses and sip, eyeing each other over the rims.

"So, you got tired of cherry girl," I say.

"Knotting a cherry stem isn't that impressive a bar trick. I can do it too."

I choke on my next sip of whisky. "You, Ryan, can knot a cherry stem with your tongue?"

"Mhmm. Hours on the road traveling, you gotta kill time somehow."

Hearing a pro athlete cop to that skill surprises and delights me.

Before I can invite him, he circles the bar and comes in beside me, crouching next to me to see what I have beneath the bar. "Nice collection. I'm from Kentucky. I know my bourbon."

"Of course you do."

"I always wanted to be a bartender."

I spread my hands. "Be my guest."

There are no seats, so I hop up on the bar.

I go fishing for a cherry, trying the stem thing for myself while he works.

"This is hard," I complain.

He holds out a hand, and I pass him one. He pops it in his mouth and, a moment later, puts the stem—tied—in his hand.

"No way."

He holds out a drink.

"For me?"

"Yeah. You've been making them all night."

I take a sip. "That's actually good."

I'm watching the way the low lights play over his face. I take another delicious sip, almost moaning before I swallow.

I shift to one side, planting my palm on the wood bar as I cock my head. My skirt's riding up, but I don't bother fixing it. The alcohol is buzzing in my veins, and I'm not sure when the walls I put up started to fall, but I'm more relaxed than I've been all night.

I take another cherry but drop it. He catches it in front of me, my knees bumping his chest when he straightens.

"Good tongue. Good hands. Anything else you're good at?" I ask lightly as I take the cherry, biting off the fruit and dropping the stem on the bar.

I don't even mean it like that. Or hell, maybe I do.

Because when Ryan's eyes glint, it lights something up in me.

"You want to find out?" His voice is playful and a little rough, as if the idea of me finding out exactly how good he is turns him on.

Heat floods me.

How long has it been since I've hooked up with someone?

This year has been crazy with the team's success. I've worked a wild number of hours. The idea of one wild night with the hottest rookie in basketball is a tempting fantasy.

Except it could get complicated.

It won't, I insist. *It's only physical.*

Ryan sways toward me, or maybe it only feels that way.

We both look down. My hand's fisted in the front of his sweater, and I have no damn clue how that happened. Somehow my knees have slipped farther apart, my skirt halfway up my thighs now.

My next inhale is shallow, the air rough in my throat.

The music changes to a sultry track.

I've flirted with the idea of hooking up with players. Even done it a couple of times. But one time, I let myself get in too deep, and it burned me.

Now, I have a rule: no hooking up with someone as central to my business as a member of the Kodiaks' starting five.

This bar is the team, and while sex is only sex, it's a bad fucking idea to imagine it with him.

"It's a bad idea," I murmur.

"Probably," he agrees.

I inch closer to the edge of the bar. Ryan's hand finds my knee, and the lightest pressure of his thumb just inside has my body lighting up.

"But it is Christmas," I add under my breath.

"Mistletoe and all." His nose bumps mine as he nods.

Heat crackles between us. I want him so badly I can taste him.

It's only one night. That vow has me teetering on the edge.

"All right, Rookie. Show me what you've got."

Triumph flares in his dark eyes.

His hand travels up my leg. I'm sliding closer to the edge, his other hand on my hip. The one up my leg finds the top of my tights with stars on them. He yanks them down.

My fingers splay over his sweater, and I wish I could feel his skin underneath, the hard ridges and smooth muscles. But he takes my hand and places it on the bar next to me, nudging me backward. His fingers find the edge of my thong, then slip beneath, and he groans. His thumb strokes right where I need him most.

My head falls back, my spine arching. I can't even play it cool because he's playing with me as though it's the only thing he's ever wanted to do.

I realize the curtains are open.

"No one's out there," he says, reading my mind.

"How the hell do you know?"

"You can't get a car down this street. I had to park three blocks away and walk."

I should be doing something with that information, but I can't because the ache he's creating and solving all at once is more important than thinking.

Maybe more than breathing.

"Fuck, you're tight," he says with total satisfaction.

He presses another finger inside, changing up the rhythm to a slow drag that destroys me.

My body pulls tight. I can't lie back here. I shift off my elbows, my hands finding his shoulders.

He lowers his face, lips parted. He's breathing heavily too. "Sierra..."

I don't kiss him. Instead, I bury my face in his sweater and grip him harder as my body tightens.

He doesn't say anything, but his thumb presses harder, rubbing little circles right above where he's slowly pumping in and out of me. My nails find his neck, digging in hard. His breath is shaky, but he doesn't resist.

When I come, it's more like shattering. The

tension I've been carrying for way too long feels as if it all releases at once, like a star detonating into space. Pleasure rushes through every nerve. Tremors rack my body before dissipating into the air around us.

Ryan withdraws, and I realize I'm still clutching him.

His eyes flash, and his hands go for his belt. I can't tell if I'm helping or slowing him down, but we get his zipper down.

Ryan fishes in his wallet for a condom, and the sound of the foil crinkling when he locates one is pure relief. I take the package wordlessly and tear into it, setting the condom on his hard cock before rolling it down.

And shit, he's big, though I'm not about to make his ego swell by saying the words.

I encourage him between my thighs, the press of him where his fingers just left feeling too sensitive. But there's no time to slow down because he's sinking inside me. The stretch, the burn, the slide sends every nerve in me crackling with heat.

This is definitely the most fun I've had on this bar.

Whatever exhaustion I was feeling an hour

ago feels light-years away. There's only this desire, this need, this pleasure.

He rocks his hips against me. "Fuck," he groans against my neck. "You feel so damned good."

I shift on my elbows to meet him.

The drag of our bodies, the heat, is addictive. In a few short strokes, his breath is shallow, my heart hammering.

"Oh, shit. I can't wait…"

His grunt is low and guttural, coupled with the feel of him clenching. One of my hands digs into his arm, the other sliding between us. I'm still on edge from the last time, so I get myself there, my fingers digging into his muscles as I ride it out.

My head falls back against the bar, my eyes closing. I weigh a thousand pounds, and it's glorious.

The music has stopped. I'm not sure when or what the last song was.

At some point, Ryan's murmur comes from over me. "I'm sorry."

"For what?" I laugh, stretching both arms overhead. My fingers brush glassware as my eyes blink open.

The sight is a good one—Ryan silhouetted by the lights over the bar. His hair is spiky from my fingers, his million-dollar smile on full display.

"For how fast that was," he admits. "I'm not usually... but you were..."

I chuckle. "That's the best compliment I've gotten all night."

10

RYAN

"Rookie!" Snow hits the back of my head. "You good?"

I adjust the tree in my grip to look at Miles. "Yeah. Why?"

"You stopped walking, and you have this dumb expression on your face."

I force my feet to move again as we head back toward the cabin.

My mind is still back there in the snow.

Last Christmas, I was at the bar with the guys after the game. I did Sierra a solid, then on impulse doubled back to make sure she was okay. I was not expecting the hot-as-hell fever dream that went down after.

Had I imagined it more than once? Sure.

But the reality of Sierra was a thousand times better.

The past twelve months, I've been thinking about how right it felt to be with her but telling myself she promptly forgot our hookup, that it didn't stick with her like it did me.

Now, I know that's not true.

I've had a crush on the team's unofficial bartender for a long time. Everyone jokes about players wanting to hook up, and sure, it's easier than keeping a serious relationship going given the demanding schedule.

Somehow, though, all I wanted from Sierra was more.

More physical, but also more of her laugh. More of her smile. More of the kindness she thinks she hides behind toughness.

I kissed Sierra because hearing her talk about other holidays, seeing how cute she was, I couldn't keep my hands off her.

When I touched her today, our chemistry was every bit as alive as it was a year ago. She responded just as enthusiastically.

But the moment I press for more, she pumps the brakes.

Probably because Sierra has a line of guys and girls every night who'd love to get with her. Why should she treat me any differently?

"You and Nova disappeared earlier," I say.

"That a question?" Clay grunts.

"No. You got any tips?" I hear myself ask. "About women, I mean. Because you guys seem really good."

Miles is on the other side, Jay behind me.

"Who've you got your eye on?" Jay asks.

"No one," I lie. Sierra would gut me if she knew I was asking for advice about her. "I think I want that—the right girl."

"You're twenty-three."

"Twenty-four now," I correct.

"Right. You still wouldn't know the right girl if she walked up to you in your jersey."

"That's bullshit." I say it louder than I mean to and feel all the eyes turn toward me. "Just because you've got a few years on me, you think you know your mind better than I know mine."

"You stick around the league a few years and you realize everything happens at a different pace. It's like getting on a ride at the fair. Takes you two seasons just to get your footing," Miles offers.

"It's hard," Clay says finally. "Basketball and the right person."

"But?"

"But you do it because when you meet her, you can't imagine not doing it."

"What about you?" I ask Miles.

"With Brooke, I know we could each survive on our own. But we don't want to. She makes the highs and the lows better," he says. "On the good days, there's always someone to celebrate with. But on the shitty days, I have someone to laugh with."

I can picture being that.

"Why don't you ask me?" Jay protests.

"Last I looked, you don't have a girl."

Miles bursts out laughing.

"I could."

A muffled sound from behind us has me looking around.

"Do you hear it too?" I ask.

"No—wait, yeah." We put down the tree and listen.

"It's probably Trista. She heard you saying

you want a girlfriend, and she's running over here."

"It doesn't sound human," Jay decides nervously.

"Probably nothing." The cabin's fifty meters up ahead, and I nod to the tree. "Let's get this inside."

11

MILES

Carrying the tree back to the cabin through the deep snow is a new kind of gym workout. I'm silently impressed Ryan cut down a tree, though I'm not about to give him props.

But the guy is distracted. I'd swear it's by whatever he and Sierra were talking about when we showed.

I'm no matchmaker—Brooke's more that person between the two of us—but I'm down for a little gossip. It wasn't weird to see Sierra show up here, because she's in the group chat and often at parties and hangs with the girls.

Something's up.

I'd like to see Ryan, in all his eagerness and cockiness, laid flat over a girl. That would make my holiday.

Jay goes in the door first. The branches are covered with snow, and as we get the tree inside, snow flicks off the branches and onto the floor.

Chloe screeches. "You're making a mess!"

"It's worth it, Chlo," I say.

The inside of the cabin is cozy after the chill from outside.

Not going to lie, Ryan picked a good spot. When he proposed sneaking away for a couple days before the Christmas game, it seemed like an easy idea. But the small cabin, as tricked out as it is, was not what I expected.

I'm starting to appreciate it.

"You couldn't get something smaller?" Chloe demands as we carry the tree to the corner.

"This is the one," Ryan insists.

I know the feeling. When you know, you know.

My gaze lands on the woman curled up by the fire in a pink sweater and shiny yoga pants, my dog in her lap and a magazine spread in front of her.

Brooke has been it for me since almost the second I laid eyes on her.

I've known her since college. I got drafted partway through and she was just starting, but because I played near her school, her brother asked me to look out for her.

Being Jay's teammate and best friend made it forbidden as hell that I had a thing for her.

Her warm eyes, her drive, her sense of humor. Her killer curves and the way she dances. I love everything about her.

"Whatcha reading, Princess?"

There's a stack of wedding magazines on the table next to her, so I know what she's got, but I want to see it for myself.

Now, the big diamond on her finger is evidence of the fact I shake myself with when I wake up every morning: Brooke agreed to marry me.

It's going to be the perfect ending to our story... if she'd only agree to a date.

I lean over the spread and eye the pages, expecting to see wedding dresses and flower arrangements. I was glad to see she brought a bunch of magazines with her and hoped she'd use this time to settle on some decisions. She's the one into design and fashion, and it makes her happy, so I'll get my girl anything she wants.

"What the...? Cookies?" I ask, surprised to see baked goods on the pages rather than white gowns and flowers.

"And coffee cakes." She thumbs through the pages with silver holiday-decorated nails.

"Since when do you bake?"

"I'm an excellent window shopper."

"I thought you were looking at wedding stuff."

Brooke lowers the magazine. "I *am* looking at those things."

She cocks her head at me. In her lap, my Frenchie mimics her.

God, she's got him wrapped around her finger.

I lean on the chair and bend down, brushing my lips over hers. When she softens, my hand tangles in her hair and I kiss her deeper.

"When are you tying the knot?" Atlas calls.

I pull back, waiting on her to answer.

"We can't book a venue until I know lead times on my dress."

I swallow my sigh at Brooke's words. Since I proposed, I've been wanting to get this thing done. The conversation with the guys outside reminded me how important this is—how important she is.

The sheer difficulty of being a top athlete and maintaining a healthy relationship... It's not fair to my girl how much I'm gone, the demands on my time, all the nights I come home beat.

"Come on. Let's go bake something," I say.

"Really?" Her nose scrunches up.

I lift her chin with a finger. "What did you have in mind?"

"Let's go skating."

Nova agrees to join, plus Chloe.

We get dressed for the weather and head outside, Waffles yipping happily at our heels.

Brooke makes a beeline for the shed, where Ryan said he found his saw. The outbuilding only has two pairs of skates, but...

"Toboggans!" Brooke exclaims as she spots the two sleds. "There's a hill on the other side of the rink."

"You'd rather fly down a hill than skate?" Nova asks.

"Have we met?! Obviously."

They laugh, and I carry the toboggans that way. Fortunately, they're both wider than children's ones, though it'll be a tight fit.

"Clay didn't want to come?" Brooke teases as we walk. The fur lining the hood of her jacket sways in the wind.

"Skating isn't his thing. There's a limit to his whimsy," Nova says.

"You guys know each other so well," Chloe observes. "I never thought I'd see him find his person—well, other than himself."

The women all laugh.

"Yeah. He's definitely used to going it alone. I try to show him it's more fun together." Nova's sweet face is bright.

"What's up with Ryan and Sierra?" Brooke asks. "I think he has a thing for her. He always looks for her at the bar."

"I mean... she's the bartender," I reply.

"Does he hook up on the road?"

I zip my lips. "Not talking. Bear code."

Three pairs of eyes stare me down. Chloe's unsurprised, Nova's disappointed, and Brooke's like, *Are you fucking kidding me?*

"But..." I relent a little. "I think he misses having someone to call him on his bullshit."

We get to the top of the hill and peer down. The sun glints off the snow, and more snow is coming down.

"Well, only one thing to do now." Brooke perches at the front of the sled, gathering Waffles into her lap. Both of them looks up at me.

I put my hands on the back of the toboggan.

Brooke twists around. "You don't think all three of us will fit?"

"We're damn well going to try."

I start running and pushing, then jump onto the toboggan. Brooke throws up her hands and my dog yips.

We slide down the hill, faster than I expect. The whoosh of wind on my face feels good. So does having her in front of me.

In the league, guys think of me as the fun one. But Brooke makes it all magic. She's the best sidekick at a party or partner in crime for a prank.

The second run, we lean the wrong way, and we go sprawling.

I land next to her in a pile. She's grinning.

"I love you, Princess."

"I love you."

"Want to go back and bake cookies?"

"Great."

But I swear her smile dims a little, and I wish I knew why.

Brooke

I TAKE Waffles back to the cabin, then strip out of my jacket and boots before heading to the kitchen. I pull out baking supplies from under the counter, plus mixing bowls. There's a bag of giant candy canes Miles brought. I take one.

Is this really who we are? Cozy cottage baking people?

For the longest time, I wanted a man who saw me and had my back through everything.

I found him. He'd been there the whole time.

My fiancé, the all-star of the league and my fantasies. All the memories I have of secret hookups and longing looks and sexy road trips.

It's stupid to wonder, but what if the tension, the sneaking around, was part of the fun? Will that go away once we tie the knot?

On impulse, I pull my boots back on. I return to the shed and tug open the door. Inside, the sunlight falls over Miles resetting the sleds on a shelf.

"I love you. I love our life."

He turns, meeting my gaze. "Me too."

"I don't want things to get… boring."

"Boring?" he echoes, his dark brows shooting up under the thick fall of hair.

"There's always been so much tension between us. Fire. Chaos." I shrug helplessly.

His gaze drops to my hand and the candy cane in it. "You think we'll bake peppermint chocolate chip cookies and all of a sudden it'll be dull?"

"You're making fun of me," I grumble, folding my arms.

His eyes crinkle. "C'mere."

I oblige, stomping across the floor to him.

He's really handsome even when he's laughing at me.

"You remember the time you took me shopping for your sorority retreat?" His hands reach for the front of my pants. "You were helping me get dressed."

"What's your point?"

"My point is, all I could think about was how it would feel to fuck you in that dressing room."

The memory has arousal tingling through me. "But that's because we couldn't. It was hot because we knew it wasn't an option."

His eyes dance. "Turn around."

With a suspicious look, I comply.

He finds the waist of my yoga pants and tugs them down over my hips. The cold air hits my thighs and makes me shiver.

"I used to think about you all the time," he says. "When I was in practice. You were Jay's little sister, and it was forbidden as hell. I knew it, but I couldn't stop wanting you." Every word turns me on more. Especially when he says, "Lean on the sled."

The toboggan is in front of me, and I place

my hands on the smooth wood. "What are you doing?"

I feel his hand on my lower back.

He takes the candy cane lying next to me.

"Boring things. The kind we're gonna do when we're married."

His fingers brush my panties, the cold air making me extra sensitive. Then he sucks on the candy cane, releasing it with a pop.

Miles's hand finds my shoulders and gently pushes me down. "When we started hanging out, I thought it would be easier. Being around you. Like it would take the edge off the way I wanted you. Instead, having you up close only made me want you more. I wanted you in my place, my life."

My throat is dry, every inch of me craving his touch. "Not your bed?"

"I pictured you and me a thousand places. Bed didn't even crack the top ten."

I feel the poke of the firm object where I'm wet. It's wet too, and it slides in.

"Ohhh."

The shed creaks with a gust of wind, and I tense, looking at the door. "Someone could come in."

"Too exciting for you?" he teases.

He works the candy cane in and out until I'm pushing back, needing more.

"Fuck, you look good," Miles mutters.

Finally, he pulls out the candy cane. The wrapper crinkles, and I twist to look at him in time to see him discard the plastic and hold it out to me.

Miles's hands go to his belt, but he waits me out. When he works his zipper down, I can see the massive bulge in his shorts.

I take the candy cane from him and put it on my tongue. The minty flavor fills my tastebuds.

Miles presses against me where I'm wet.

I moan a little around the end of the candy cane.

"More," I say.

"You first."

I suck on the candy cane.

He presses deeper into me.

Fuck.

"Miles…"

His finger rubs my clit, little strokes exactly the way I need them. My breathing gets shallow.

"That's it, Princess." He rewards my responsiveness with more of him.

Soon he's pumping in and out, deep enough that he slaps against my skin.

"I'll never get tired of the ways I want you and the things I want to experience with you." He says it like a promise, and it's everything I need.

My fingers grip the edge of the shelf. "I can't..."

The reverberations start deep in my stomach. My body tightens, waves of pleasure rippling through me.

I come in a sweaty, shaking pile. He's already groaning against my ear.

"You're so beautiful. Never dreamed life could get this good. Now and always."

I reach back, my limp fingers finding the back of his tense neck to hold him closer.

He's close. I can feel it.

I squeeze one more time, my nails digging lightly into his neck, and that's all it takes.

Miles roars and spills deep inside me. It's almost as satisfying to feel him lose control, to know that I'm the one who gets to make the guy the world knows as an easygoing player come totally unhinged.

"Admit it," I pant when we can breathe again. "The tobogganing was better than the baking."

Miles chuckles, tracing a line down my back that he follows with his mouth. "You might be right about that, Princess."

12

SIERRA

"This is impressive," Nova says as she hangs snowflakes on the far side of the tree. "Ryan cut this down?"

"He almost took me out with it," I respond.

Nova found a box of ornaments in a closet, and she and I have been decorating the tree Ryan brought in. I pick a little wooden bear out of the box and hang it.

"Sounds like an exciting date." She smiles as she hangs a wreath on the other side.

"I wouldn't call it that."

Except for the part when I sprawled on top of him as though I was experiencing hypothermia and needed his body heat for survival.

That part was definitely date-like.

The smell of cookies drifts from the oven. Gooey chocolate and vanilla. My stomach growls in anticipation, and I consider pausing my current work to ambush the treats.

The guys are looking around in the woods to see if they can find the source of the noises we've been hearing all weekend. Secretly, I think they want to have a snow fight.

As for me? I've been thinking about that kiss all afternoon.

How it felt to have Ryan's mouth on mine… The look in his eyes said he's not letting me off the hook this time.

I'm starting to wonder if I even want to be let off.

"How well do you know Ryan?" I hear myself ask.

"We came to Denver around the same time," Nova says.

She picks up another ornament, a little bell, sizing up the remaining available branches. "He was Clay's rookie first year. They're pretty close. His family usually comes for Christmas whether he's playing or not, but I didn't hear about them visiting this year.

"His sisters both play sports too. I remember him going to support their games. One time he wore this T-shirt from their high school to media. It broke the fundraising page."

Of course he's kind and funny and reps his sisters' high school teams.

It's easy to see Ryan only as a player, but there's so much more to him.

Not that I'm interested in the "more."

The fact that I want him so badly is clouding my judgment.

Maybe last year wasn't a mistake. That's why I keep thinking about it.

It was unplanned, a surprise. But maybe there's something to this holiday spirit thing.

We finish up the tree as Brooke calls from the kitchen, "Who wants a cookie?"

"I'll take two," Nova says as we both bound to the island where Brooke's setting out a big plate. Nova eyes the tree critically. "What do you think? Is it done?"

"It's perfect," Brooke says.

I bite into my cookie, and it tastes even better than it looks.

I'm still thinking about it the rest of the afternoon and over dinner.

We laugh our way through the gift swap, stealing one another's draws mercilessly. The most triumphant person is Brooke, who got Miles to steal for her a little golden bear figurine I found at a flea market and thought would match the guys' trophy collections. The moment she saw it, she decided it would be perfect to hang her non-basketball-related jewelry on.

The best prize went to the misshapen mug made by Jay in his pottery class. He claimed it was "art" and signed the bottom accordingly. When Chloe tried drinking out of it, champagne dripped down her chin until we were all cracking up.

I scored a wall calendar featuring squirrels in tiny disco outfits posed like a Studio 54 fever dream.

Ryan nabbed an "Influencer in the Wild" starter pack featuring a ring light keychain, dry shampoo, and a bottle of coconut water (for his "Hot Girl Walk" hydration).

We're all sprawled around the living room when someone's phone beeps loudly. Then again.

Chloe leaps up from the chair she's lying across. "No. No, this can't be happening."

"What's wrong?" Jay's instantly alert.

She looks up from her phone. "They've closed the main road into town. The few inches of snow got upgraded to more than a foot."

"Meaning...?" Nova asks.

"Meaning the only basketball the Kodiaks are going to be playing tomorrow is here."

We exchange looks.

I cross to the window and peek outside. The snow is piling up.

"Sure looks pretty from in here," Nova offers, peering over my shoulder.

"What are we going to do?"

Ryan holds up a hand. "Don't worry. I've got it covered."

He disappears upstairs.

While he's gone, Chloe starts making calls on her phone.

"And voila!"

Ryan reappears at the top of the stairs, and I blink up at him.

He's wearing bright red swimming trunks with cars on them and nothing else.

"How is that supposed to solve the road closure?" Chloe sighs, clicking off.

I take in his muscled body in all its glory, greedily drinking him in. Whatever he's up to, I feel like it would solve a lot of my problems.

"We've got a hot tub, and it would be a crime not to use it. Let's go."

~

Ryan

THE HOT TUB is supposed to fit twelve, but by the time I get outside in my towel and spot Clay, Nova, Jay, and Atlas in there, it's getting cozy. Probably because three of the bodies are pro athletes the size of trucks.

"You coming in?" Jay calls from the far side. The shortest of us at six foot, the water reaches most of the way up his chest.

"Fuck yeah. I'm shrinking every second I'm out here."

Nova shifts into Clay's lap to make more room, which he doesn't look at all upset by.

I hang my towel on a hook with a pile of

them as I hear the door at my back. Miles and Brooke appear in their robes.

"You seen Chloe and Sierra?" I ask.

"Think they're still upstairs. Maybe talking," Miles says, helping his girl as they ditch their robes and climb into the hot tub.

The storm hit worse than anticipated. With the road back to town is closed, Chloe's freaking out over how to get us back.

The fact is we're stranded here for the moment.

I get that it's a big deal if we're not in Denver for the Christmas game, but I'm selfishly hoping they're talking about the fact that I kissed Sierra this afternoon.

That's sure as hell what I've been thinking about every second since.

"Nice shorts," Brooke calls from behind me.

"Thanks." I glance at the red fabric with race cars on it.

Going back inside to check on the girls seems too obvious. Resigned, I rub my hands together for warmth and take the stairs up to the tub.

The water is hot and delicious.

I take a seat on the edge closest to the stairs, letting my legs adjust to the temperature.

Laughter at my back makes me turn.

Chloe's first, carrying her e-reader and bag.

"Where's your phone?" Jay teases.

"Ran out of battery. It's charging in the living room." She frowns.

Neither of them is wearing a robe, not that my teammate seems to mind from the way he's looking at his ex-girlfriend.

I can't focus on that because I'm watching Sierra in a black two-piece. The suit hugs her hips and breasts. I get a long look at the soft curve of her stomach, the indent of her back, her toned thighs from hours spent on her feet.

"Shit, it's cold!" she exclaims, wrapping her arms around herself.

She's got ink all kinds of places, mostly black like her hair. I want to know every tattoo on her body. To learn why she got each one.

Warm water splashes the back of my head.

"Be chivalrous, man," Atlas goads.

I hold out a hand to help Chloe up into the hot tub. She climbs in, eyeing the space to find a spot.

"Need somewhere to sit, Chlo?" Jay asks. "There's room over here."

She reluctantly wedges in on the far side, holding her tablet carefully out of the water.

"I'll wait," Sierra says, wrapping her arms around her.

Protests go up around the tub.

"No way. Get in."

She takes my hand. If there was any doubt about the chemistry between us, it's gone now. Her eyes lock with mine, and it all comes back in a rush.

Learning her tattoos can wait. I want her against me. Every damned inch of her skin on every inch of mine. I'll wrap her around me twice.

"See? There's no room," she's saying.

"Here." I try to shift sideways so she's on one side of my calves. Sierra shifts to the edge of the seat.

My knees move automatically to either side of her. Suddenly, there's room for her to sit back between my legs. It's not as close as Nova in Clay's lap or Brooke in Miles's, but it's still cozy.

Sierra's eyes find mine as she twists to look

over her shoulder. "You aren't in the hot tub," she points out.

Fuck cozy. It's as if she's on her knees in front of me. Only a visual I've had a thousand times over the past year.

"It's fine," I grit out. "Nice suit."

"Thanks. It was lucky this was wedged in a pocket of my suitcase from whenever my last trip was, or I would've been skinny dipping."

Well, there's an idea that has my dick paying attention.

Be cool.

"Tell me you're not getting weather updates on that," Miles calls to Chloe.

"I'm reading a book."

"What book?"

"A romance."

Nova leans in. "Oooh, say more."

"The couple has a one-night stand, then he comes back into her life way later."

Sierra tenses between my legs, her shoulders brushing my thighs.

"You got a matching race car bed to go with those shorts?" Sierra whispers.

I lean toward her, close enough that I catch her floral scent over the chlorine of the hot tub.

"You keep talking about my bed," I say under my breath, my hands resting lightly on her shoulders, "I'm gonna have to give you a tour."

Her skin is soft. I can't resist stroking the back of her shoulders with my thumbs.

She arches a little, a small adjustment only I notice.

"That a promise?" she murmurs.

Her lips part as I release her, but it's my turn to be left speechless.

After a year of second guessing and wanting, my literal dream girl is picking up what I'm putting down.

Fuck. It's on.

Will it make me a bad host if I grab her and carry her out of the hot tub and up to my room this second?

Might be worth it.

"You guys had the best meeting story," Chloe's saying to Nova as I try to focus.

"Did you ever tell me?" Sierra asks.

"It was on a plane." Nova smiles, exchanging a look with Clay. "I was coming for my sister's wedding. She booked me in first class. I was already nervous and the flight was running late, and this massive guy with tattoos and headphones and 'fuck off' energy comes and sits next to me. They were holding the plane for him, and I had no idea." Everyone's cracking up, and even Sierra's shoulders are rocking. "He was a total dick."

"I wasn't a dick." Clay brushes Nova's hair off her shoulder, rubbing her neck.

"It fucked him up every bit as much," Jay says. "The next day, I could tell something was wrong."

"How about you guys?" Sierra asks Brooke.

"We don't need to hear this," Jay protests. "That's my little sister. She was in college."

Brooke and Miles exchange a look.

"I'm going to throw this at your head, man," Jay promises on a groan, reaching for Chloe's tablet.

"It's not yours." She resists, wrenching it back.

"What about you two?" I hear myself ask.

Jay and Chloe freeze, both caught out like deer in headlights.

"You used to date. Everyone knows it," I say.

"It was a full moon," Chloe says at last. "I

needed a save. He gave me one. Even blew off a game to do it."

"Jay blew off a game?" Miles chortles.

"She made me do a lot of things that weren't me," he says with a half smile.

Chloe's gaze lingers on Jay.

"But you guys split. How is it not awkward?" I ask.

"We work together. We've both moved on."

"So, what went wrong?" Sierra asks, and it's not unkind.

"We need the secret to lasting relationships," Nova adds.

Chloe holds up her tablet. "If I find out, I'll let you know." We all laugh. "You seeing anyone, Sierra?"

My muscles tense. I hadn't thought about the possibility that she was. Just because she came up here with us doesn't mean she couldn't be dating some other guy.

"No," she says. "I'm better off as a lone wolf."

When she says the words, I can breathe again. Except now I'm thinking about how fucking good it would feel to be the guy in her life.

To see her in the morning. To make her coffee. To pick her up after a long shift. To look up at the box during a game and see her in my jersey. To strip it off her late at night.

"You only think that because you haven't found someone worth sticking around for." I hear myself say it.

Sierra's hand on my ankle tightens. "Oh? Because the only possible reason to not be in a relationship is failing to find the right person?"

My friends and teammates exchange surprised looks.

"No, but when you find the right person, your reasons might start to look more like excuses. I've heard," I add, aware of everyone watching us.

She shifts away from me—only a few inches, but enough that I notice.

Nova lets out a little squeak. "I'm going to fall asleep if I stay in here any longer."

Clay helps her up, and she heads for the stairs.

When they make their way toward the steps, I'm still turning over what just went down and how I managed to fuck this up.

A thumping on the door makes us all jump.

I cross to it and pull it wide.

"Ryan! Oh my God, are you guys okay?"

Trista is there with another woman, both knee-deep in snow with curls sticking out from under fluffy hats.

"Uhh, yeah. I could ask you the same."

I step back to let them in. Everyone clusters around us.

"Our power went out for a few minutes, but it's back on." Trista's friend brushes snow off her hat.

Trista nods, stomping off her furry boots. "We wanted to check in with you and make sure you have what you need for the storm."

"Thanks. I think we're fine."

"Good. There were sounds in the woods on the way over."

"You shouldn't walk back alone," Nova says.

The guys look at one another. "Who wants to—"

"You should go with them, Rookie."

I cut a look back at Sierra standing on the steps.

My heart sinks.

"Great idea!" Trista cooes, already grabbing my arm in both her hands.

I'm screwed.

"You want company?" Miles offers.

"No, it's fine. You relax."

"Be careful out there. Who knows what those noises are."

My feet feel weighted to the ground as I go change and tug on my jacket. As I stomp out into the snow with the women, their perky voices filling the night, I'm still thinking of Sierra and how she volunteered me for Kodashian duty.

I'm spending the next hour at least with two women who clearly enjoy my company.

Noises are the least of my worries.

13

―――――

SIERRA

I had no idea Chloe could snore so loudly.

That's why I can't sleep. It's the only reason—and has nothing to do with being that close to Ryan in the hot tub—that my mind is still spinning.

You haven't found someone worth sticking around for.

He doesn't know anything about me. I'm taking care of myself because the one time I let myself believe I could be with someone like him, it burned me.

He's the one with women lining up around the block. Even in the wilderness, he can't get away from being famous.

We hooked up once.

And we were going to hook up again until he started acting like he knew me and what was best for me.

Ryan only saw what I wanted him to see—like all of them do.

I shove off the covers and stomp for the door. I get to the hallway, where there's no more snoring. It's mercifully quiet.

Until there's a scratching sound outside.

It's the same noise we heard in the woods earlier.

Could be anything. A squirrel.

Too big for a squirrel.

Larger animals wouldn't come around the cabin. There's no food left out, and it's winter anyway.

What if it's an intruder?

I stiffen.

My phone is on the nightstand. I go back and grab it even though there's barely any reception.

I silently pick my way down the stairs. The carpet is soft on my bare feet.

There're no more fire implements by fireplace. Did the guys take them to their rooms?

The living room is dark, only low slanted moonlight coming from one high window.

I start for the kitchen, where there are lots of sharp objects, but before I get there, the tree calls to me. There's a pointy star we never got around to putting up. I palm it.

The sounds start up again. I take a deep breath and start for the door. This energy needs to go somewhere.

The door—it's not locked.

It swings open.

My mouth goes wide, and I inhale sharply, ready to scream, ready to bring the star down on the intruder.

I swipe as hard as I can.

The weapon connects with flesh, sinking in a little.

"Oof. Shit." The intruder hisses.

That voice is familiar. Oh no…

"Ryan?!" I gasp.

"Easy, ninja." He winces as he steps inside.

I can see his outline against the snow as my eyes adjust. "What were you doing out there?!"

"Securing the perimeter."

"That's a thing you heard on TV."

He steps inside, and I shut the door, lock it,

and hit the light switch closest to the door. He peels off his jacket, probing his chest with a hand.

"Did I get you?" I feel sick. I just attacked a member of the world champion Denver Kodiaks. My dad will *kill* me.

I'll never live it down.

"You stabbed me with… the tree star. That's festive."

"You're delusional. Come on." I grab his arm and tug him toward the kitchen. I debate turning on more lights and opt for the little one over the sink by the window. "Take off your shirt."

His brows lift, but he doesn't say anything when I shoot him a dark look.

There's an angry red scrape an inch long.

"Have you had a tetanus shot?"

"Yes, doctor."

At least that's something. "Don't move."

I go to the bathroom to grab first aid supplies. In my bag, there's gauze, antiseptic, and liquid bandage.

"For a woman who claims not to care, you're very prepared," he comments when I return.

I rummage under the sink, only finding a clean dishcloth. That'll have to do.

The blood comes off in a smear, replaced with more in a couple seconds. Dammit.

"Sit down."

I grab a chair, and he sinks into it. That's not better, because we're practically at eye level now. I'm a little higher, and if I thought his face looked good from below, he's even more handsome from this new angle.

Ryan's lips are curved at the corner.

"Are you enjoying this?" I mutter.

"Being stabbed?"

Touché.

What if this doesn't stop bleeding?

I pull out my phone. No reception. Dammit.

He shuffles his feet. "So, you can use a phone, just not to contact me."

"What?"

I shove the phone back in my pocket in frustration. When I look up, he's watching, amusement blurring with something else in his dark eyes.

"After we hooked up, I figured I'd get a call. A text. Hell, a single phrase in one of the dozen conversations we've had since." His expression is surprisingly earnest and has me biting back whatever flippant comment is on the tip of my tongue.

"We had sex, Ryan. It was a one-night thing." My voice is low, but it carries in the cabin. The darkness wraps around us, the soft light from over the sink casting a warm glow over his skin. "If I hook up with a Kodiak, it can only be one time. Nothing more."

"Do you do that a lot?" There's a wary edge to his voice. Still, he doesn't seem insecure or judgmental, just as though he's trying to understand.

His honesty is why I answer the same way.

"Not really." I sigh. "Besides, I see you twice a week. I figured *you* would've said something."

"I wanted to. But at Mile High, you always have a lot of guys hitting on you, and I didn't want to come into your space and make you uncomfortable."

His thoughtfulness sets me back. Not many people think of my wants first. It has me feeling grateful and strangely self-conscious.

"I'm sorry. It was good. Really good. But..." I set the washcloth on the counter and fold my arms. "I wasn't looking to start something, and you definitely weren't."

He tilts his head. "How do you figure?"

The bleeding's slowed. I focus on that as I turn away and shake the liquid bandage. I spray it on his skin, my other hand on his shoulder to steady him—or me.

"You're a big deal. World champion. Everyone knows your face. You were in the middle of the season. You had some shit going on as a team."

"I know what was going on for me, bartender. I meant you."

I turn away and recap the liquid bandage. "The bar is everything to my dad, and the Kodiaks are everything to the bar. Getting into any kind of relationship with a player makes it messier.

"Once, I don't regret it. Twice..." I lift a shoulder. "It could mess with the dynamics of the bar."

"That's what you're worried about? The bar?"

"What else would I worry about?" Defensiveness creeps in.

"That someone could catch feelings and get hurt. That maybe it'd be you."

He says it kindly, but I scoff anyway. "Unlikely."

I go back to my work.

"It wouldn't have been twice," he offers after a minute.

"What?"

"With us." He pauses. "It would've been a hell of a lot more than twice."

My heart kicks.

He's not saying he's obsessed with me, but damn, it feels that way.

"Is that part of this lone wolf bullshit you claimed in the hot tub?" he asks. "Don't pretend that's not why you hightailed it out of there by the way."

I feel myself stiffen on instinct. "You act like you know what women want or need. I get mansplained to every day. I don't need it from you."

"So, tell me."

My mouth falls open.

"Unless it's some point of pride that you don't let anyone in. But it feels good to be known, Sierra. I play a team sport. You don't win by being an island. You win by knowing and by being known."

I sigh. "I guess when I'm around you, I'm reminded that we're not the same. You're flying private jets and signing swag, and I'm working long hours and arguing with my dad over a drinks list and new stools."

"You fit in fine."

"Do I?"

"Maybe you're right. Doesn't matter who's around, I can't seem to stop looking at you." He lets that settle in for a moment. Then he says, "You were really going to protect the whole cabin from intruders?"

"Yes. I look out for my friends." My lips twitch.

His eyes soften. "Go back to bed."

"I was going to sleep on the couch."

"Then I'll look for some clean sheets."

He starts upstairs, and I'm staring at his back as he recedes.

I have the weirdest feeling that I missed out on an opportunity.

We're not the same, but we have a connection. When I listen to a customer at the bar, it's genuine but has boundaries. This feels as though he's listening because he wants to.

I've spent time with Kodiaks for years, but Ryan's different. He's funny and fun, and when he looks at me, it feels as though he's seeing parts of me I haven't agreed to show him but I don't want to take back.

I want more. I shouldn't, but I do.

A moment later, he reappears, crooking his finger.

"Did you find any?" I ask.

"Something even better."

I follow him upstairs. Inside the linen closet is a ladder. He disappears up the ladder. I hesitate only a moment before following, curiosity getting the best of me.

My bare feet slip a little on the way up, but Ryan grabs my arm and pulls me up.

It's dark until Ryan clicks a switch and the whole place lights up with fairy lights.

It's a loft. A beautiful loft with a king bed.

"The listing said five bedrooms. I couldn't find the last one," he says.

The bed is even made up, with a fluffy gray duvet and at least ten pillows.

I have to bend at the waist so my head

doesn't hit the peaked A-frame roof, but it's worth it. I pad across the room, the boards creaking softly, until I reach the window at the end. It's round, like a porthole. Snow flurries drift across the glass, adding to the magic.

"It's the best room in the cabin," I whisper.

"It's yours," Ryan decides.

"No, I couldn't." I turn back to find him right behind me. He's crouched to fit.

"Yes, you can. I'll take the couch."

"But who'll protect the cabin?"

"Me. You're off duty, Sheriff."

I bite my cheek as I take in his stance. "This ceiling is a bit low for you."

He's close enough I can smell him, hear his low, steady breathing. "Or... the loft is mostly meant for being horizontal."

My gaze drifts past his massive body to the perfect cozy bed.

Suddenly I'm imagining us there, the things we could do with an entire night. All the things we never got to do at the bar.

"It would have been a lot more than twice." Ryan's words come back to me.

"This place feels magical. It's a different world," I say.

"Different like a world where you'd text me back after we hooked up?"

I peer back out into the snowy darkness. Ryan kneels next to me.

"What would you tell me?" He's playful but serious, his voice close to my ear.

"That it was hot," I say, my body remembering. "That I liked being with you."

"Liked the sex or the company?"

"Both," I admit.

He inches closer. I feel him do it, as though he's daring me to deny him.

I turn back to him, needing to see his face.

"I'm sorry I stabbed you." My voice is a whisper.

Our faces are inches apart. "I'm not."

He says it so matter-of-factly my mouth falls open.

"That's a stupid thing to—"

His lips brush mine.

He's warm and hard and smells like the pine trees outside, only better. His scent wraps around me. His mouth coaxes mine open, confident and persuasive.

My body lights up as if I'm a lock and he's

the key. Every inch of me throbs, aching for more of him.

It's him and me up here with no one else. There's no pretending I don't know how this will go down if I let it.

Ryan groans as though I'm the only thing he wants.

"If we do this," he breathes, "you can't pretend tomorrow that it never happened."

Everything feels so magical here. So right.

"Just kiss me, Rookie."

14

RYAN

She's warm and soft and everything.

The number of times I've imagined Sierra in my arms over the last twelve months is beyond comprehension.

My hands slip under her top to find her waist.

I want this so damn much. The feel of her, the taste, the sound.

My mouth slants across hers. She moans under me, and it lights me the fuck up.

The entire weekend has been a rehearsal for this moment. Adrenaline and desire pound in my veins. It's better than a playoff game.

The stakes have never been higher.

Her hands slide up my chest. She's confident, assured. Not trying to seduce or playing a part but genuinely wanting, and I swear I've never been touched like this.

I never want to be touched in any way that's not like this.

I start to scoop her up into my arms, but my head hits the roof. "Fuck," I curse, dropping both of us to the floor.

She's laughing at me. "You're a masochist."

"I'm not. If I bleed one more time…"

"Tonight's over?" she supplies.

I roll onto my back and look up at her, grinning from either the concussion or her.

Yeah, I'm not calling that bluff.

"Let's try that again." Her fingers thread through mine, and she tugs me toward the bed.

Hallelujah.

Her robe falls wide, exposing her thin sleep shirt.

"No shorts?" I say.

"You tell me."

She's so beautiful, her chest rising and falling with her breath, her hair loose around her shoulders.

Fuck, I'm so hard for this girl. If I had

enough brain cells left to be embarrassed, I would be.

The twinkling lights dance across her face, which is bright with desire as she reaches for me. Her fingers trail across my pecs, down my abs.

"You're really hot." She says it as though it's wildly inconvenient. "You probably get that a lot."

"I can't remember," I say honestly. Because somehow, all that matters right now is this. Here. With her.

I bend toward her, my lips claiming hers for countless minutes. Her skin is warm and smells like heaven. I need more. Need to taste all of her.

"Only had one problem with the time we hooked up," I murmur against her mouth.

"What's that?"

"It was over too fast."

My lips trail down her throat, her collar-bone. I want to find where she's sensitive. I need any advantage I can get.

I'm going to make her lose herself—to prove she was wrong to not text me for an entire year and act like this was nothing between us.

Fuck it, I'm going to make her a fan of Christmas too.

"Mmm. And how do you plan to fix that?" she teases.

I could tell her I've pictured it. That I fuck my hand and think of her. That I remember how her eyes looked, the scent of her skin, exactly what she as wearing, that little tattoo on her wrist and how badly I wanted to bite it.

She arches, encouraging me closer.

I'm only too happy to comply.

"So much I wanted to do," I murmur. "Again. Better. Slower."

My mouth lowers farther. Every inch makes her writhe.

I drag her sleep shirt up her chest. Her skin is soft and smooth, and there's a tail of a dragon tattooed down her ribcage. I trace it with my tongue.

I push the shirt up farther, revealing the curves of her full breasts. I cup one in my hand, my lips skimming the underside until I find a spot that makes her shiver. I play with her nipples, already hard despite the warmth of the loft.

Her soft moans are the best sound. My abs clench, my thighs. Every inch of me is ready to fuck her, but I'm holding back.

She shrugs out of the robe, and I get a look at what's underneath.

The thong is black lace and hugs her curvy hips and ass.

It teases me, makes me question my idea to take this so. Fucking. Slow.

I wrap my fingers in the panel, twisting, then yank down. They rip.

"Ryan!"

"Oops."

"These were expensive!"

"Then it's a good thing I signed a new contract this year." I could buy her a thousand pairs exactly like them.

She's so gorgeous like this, her skin flushed, her breasts hard, and the curve of her stomach leading down to the curve between her thighs. I shift over her.

My fingers brush the inside of her thigh. She shudders, her legs pressing together. I hold them apart and trace a finger up her slit.

She's wet, slick as though her body is already anticipating this. It's satisfying and torturous.

"Yes," she moans.

My thumb strokes across her clit, and she arches her hips. Her hand grabs for mine, and I think she's going to push me away, but she just holds me there.

"Is that how you like it?" I rub small, slow circles. Then I change things up. "Or like that?" I sink a finger inside her, pressing deep into her warmth.

God damn, she feels unreal. Her body grips me tightly, and my dick spasms hard—even before Sierra cries out a long, low moan.

She claps a hand over her mouth.

"Oops," she says, echoing me earlier.

I still inside her, laughter rocking my shoulders. "You want everyone to know how satisfied you are, I don't mind. Not one bit. Everyone deserves to have a great Christmas."

I withdraw my finger, then press it back in, watching her eyes change color as I do.

"Ryan..." She exhales hard, aroused and impatient. Her hands fist in the duvet.

"Yeah?"

"Can we get on with this?" She wrestles with her lip, her hands reaching for my pants.

"You're not used to taking it slow," I realize.

The expression on her face is enough admission.

I glance back over my shoulder at the window. It's pitch black. I'd guess midnight, give or take.

We have hours.

"I want you to touch me. I want to feel you come on my cock more than anything I've ever wanted. But first, I'm going to make you come so hard you're crying for it."

15

SIERRA

Tonight, out here in the wilderness, far from home, the snow outside wraps around us like a cocoon.

My skin burns everywhere the air touches it, as if steam could rise off me like it did the hot tub earlier.

Ryan's over me, his body almost laughably perfect. His shoulders are round, his biceps flexing. There are more muscles than I can name.

The little fairy lights glint behind him, forming a halo around his body.

But it's his focus that has me feeling as though I'm in for it. I'm not sure I'll survive tonight. The way he touches me as if I'm the most beautiful thing he's ever seen is getting to me. It's hard to keep him at a distance when it feels as if he's crawling inside my skin.

Especially when he says, "I'm going to make you come so hard you're crying for it."

Ryan got even hotter in the last year.

I don't want to fight with him. I want him, want everything he can give me tonight even if I know tomorrow it'll have to go back to the way things were.

"Relax," Ryan insists.

There's nowhere to put my hands. I trail the fingers of one over the duvet.

He grins and returns to work. His fingers are wicked and so damn big. He pumps in and out of me, slow strokes that hit me in so many right places I didn't know I had.

His thumb brushes my clit with impossible lightness.

It should be barely noticeable.

It's the only thing I can think about.

"Damn, you're good at that." My voice trembles at the edges.

"That's it," he murmurs. "You feel so perfect."

His praise lights me up. My hand fists in his

hair, the strands soft and silky against my damp palm. I grind my hips harder against him.

My palm finds my breast, rubbing and kneading. I do come, my core tightening around him. Every part of me shudders and he keeps stroking, drawing it out of me. Then I collapse back against the sheets.

"Stop," I pant.

"Sure. Once you come again," he says agreeably.

Ryan shifts, lowering his face between my thighs.

If his fingers were giving, his mouth is greedy. He licks at my skin, sucking and pumping until I'm a writhing mess.

The next climax comes even faster.

I'm satisfied but unsatisfied too. I shift up onto my elbows, gasping for air.

He's right there, his mouth damp and his eyes bright. "You're so perfect."

My heart kicks. He means in bed, not that it matters right now.

I stroke a hand across his chest, loving how the muscles flex under his smooth skin as I slide down. When I get to his abs, his mouth falls open on a tight exhale. My hand slips under the waist of his pants and wraps around him. He's huge and hard, already leaking.

That he wants me this badly is such a trip.

"I'm impressed you lasted, Rookie," I say lightly.

He chuckles. "I'll keep you up all night."

I play with the head of him the way he played with me. He presses into my hand, his eyes falling shut.

"Looking forward to it." I lift my hips to brush across him, both of us groaning now.

"Shit." He freezes over me. "Condom." Ryan looks around us.

"Downstairs."

He pulls on his pants and heads for the ladder.

Watching him leave has my chest tightening. It's stupid, but I had gone all in on the idea that it's only him and me here, that nothing in the world can touch us.

"Come back," I whisper right before he disappears.

Ryan stills, twisting back to look at me, cocking his head in surprise before I watch him slip out of sight.

It's crazy how much of the good vibes evaporate. Even when I turn toward the window, watching the snow drift by, I still feel his absence.

Minutes pass. I'm lying in bed, my thumbs stroking my stomach absently.

What if he doesn't come back? What if he forgets or loses interest?

I crawl toward the opening in the floor, leaning down. I'm straining to hear—footsteps, anything.

It's quiet.

He's probably gone to bed.

Except... suddenly there are voices.

Ryan's.

Then Jay's.

We're so busted.

I lean farther over, trying to make out the words. I can't tell what they're saying, but the tone is light.

He's not coming back. There's no way.

Disappointment slams into me. I crawl back to the bed. The sheets feel cooler than they did when I was sharing them.

It shouldn't be a big deal. The bed is soft and decadent. My bones feel lighter than they did this afternoon. I'm in a beautiful cabin and can get a good sleep.

Even if I am sleeping alone.

I hunker down on my side, tugging the duvet around me. I try to shut my eyes, pretending I can sleep when all I want is to go downstairs and drag Ryan back up here.

A creaking sound has me blinking my eyes open, looking over my shoulder.

Ryan's head appears, then the rest of him.

"You came back," I say.

"It'd take a lot more than running into my teammate to keep me away from you." His grin makes my chest expand.

"You got one?"

His hand disappears into the pocket of his pants. He shifts over me and presses a packet onto my stomach.

Then another.

Then another.

I laugh quietly. "You have a lot of confidence in yourself."

"Give me tonight and you will too."

I glance down at the packets and raise a brow. "Christmas colors?"

"And flavors." He lifts the first one. "Candy cane."

"God. What else is there? Eggnog? Holly?"

"Holly's poisonous."

"Please tell me there's no Christmas pudding."

He smirks. "You're the holiday grinch. I'm going to change your mind from the inside out."

"I guess it would be unkind not to let you try."

"That's the spirit." He grabs my ass, and I swear I still feel his fingers inside me. "Now flip over."

16

SIERRA

I feel as though I got hit by a truck.

A massive, beautiful truck.

One that's still at the crime scene, judging by the soft breathing inches from my ear.

Little dust specks drift through the sunlight in the window. The scents of wood and Ryan fill my senses.

The pillow is soft under my cheek as I roll toward him.

I'm not a big sleepover girl, especially with guys. This one fills the entire bed in a way that should be annoying.

Every shift of my body ignites a vivid

memory, as though despite the low lighting and muffled sounds of the cabin, I'm ready to soak in each moment.

Ryan kissing me, touching me, moving with me.

Last year's hookup was good.

This was a damned revelation.

He's really good in bed. It's such an understatement I nearly laugh.

But more than that, the things he said, the way he acted, made me feel as though he was genuinely in this for more than one night.

Am I?

I can't be.

Except... he makes me want to.

I wonder what it would be like to wake up in my bed with him next to me. To meet up with him when we're both done work, to take a hot bath and talk about each other's days and have the kind of slow sex that leaves marks. To hang out in public in that easy way Clay and Nova or Miles and Brooke do.

That was never something I aspired to, but now I'm questioning whether I was too quick to dismiss it.

I glance over my shoulder. There's a trail of

clothes along the floorboards of the loft. I creep toward the window, carefully picking up one piece after another.

He doesn't even snore.

I have to get out of here. The sentence rises up, and as much as I want to stay, I know it's true.

Getting down the ladder is trickier than getting up, but I make it. Once I get to the second floor, the scent of coffee drifts up from downstairs. I get a robe from my room—Chloe's up already, shit—and head down to the kitchen.

Brooke's there, moving around the kitchen and pulling down mugs. Nova lifts the coffee pot in one hand.

No Chloe.

Did she notice I left last night? I sure as hell hope not.

"There she is," Brooke calls.

"Please tell me there's enough for me," I say.

"There's enough for everyone." Nova pours into mugs, and I shift onto a stool on the opposite side of the island.

"Everyone?" I ask.

"Guys are still asleep. They can make another pot."

I blink, sleepiness catching up to me.

"Yesterday was fun," Nova says.

"Getting snowed in isn't so bad after all," I say.

"It's definitely not," Brooke decides.

Nova nods. "Chloe's trying to figure out what's happening with the game."

Hopefully, she's distracted enough by that she's not thinking about me.

"The league is freaking out. We can't reschedule the game. TV commitments are locked in and tickets are sold and..." Chloe's voice comes from behind me, and we all turn to face her. "Whose bed did you sleep in last night?"

"There's a loft." I try to sound cool. "I found it last night while looking for sheets for the couch."

"So, you slept in this loft?"

"Alone?" Brooke asks.

Nova smacks her in the arm. "Brooke!"

"What?! It's a legit question. The only one that has permeated my pre-caffeine haze." Her mug goes to her lips, and she watches me over it.

"Anyone want mimosas?" I ask.

Sure enough, there's happy assent.

Saved by champagne and OJ.

I grab a bottle out of the fridge and the pitcher of juice. "Nova, can you find champagne flutes?"

"Yes! I spotted some in the cabinet yesterday."

I pop the cork and start to pour.

"No champagne for me. Just OJ," Nova murmurs.

"Still not sleeping?" Brooke asks, sympathetic.

"Hmm? I slept great," Nova blinks, caught out. "I mean…"

We gasp. "Are you…?"

She beams. "I just took a test. It's early yet, and we've been trying for a while, so I don't want to get our hopes up. I haven't told Clay, but I was going to tomorrow."

"Whatever happens, we love you and so does Clay," Brooke says.

"And today is worth celebrating," Chloe adds.

We all clink glasses. This is friendship. This is what it's about.

Except... they all have a reason to be in the group. I know we've clicked the last while, but if I left, I wouldn't have them. Wouldn't have this.

There's a knot starting between my shoulder blades.

"Can we see it?" Brooke asks after we've each taken a sip.

"See what?"

"This loft." Brooke's eyes gleam, and she starts for the stairs.

I didn't want to do this. Hooking up with the Kodiaks' star rookie could cause all kinds of problems for the bar, for our friend group, for me.

Ryan appears at the top of the steps.

The knot evaporates... or it's eclipsed by the way my heart thuds against my ribs.

It's a response to the man who gave me multiple orgasms—not because of how thoughtful he is, how I'm wondering if he'd actually cook for me on Valentine's Day and how much I'd like it if he did.

Isn't it?

"Sierra said she found a loft last night," Brooke says.

He looks between us. "Oh yeah?"

I take another sip of my mimosa, the bubbles dancing on my tongue making me feel almost as alive as how it feels to be under his gaze.

Ryan's wearing gray sweatpants, and his shirt's in his hand. He pulls it on.

I can't look away.

"You have a little..." Brooke points at the corner of my mouth.

I swat at her hand.

A burst of activity at the top of the stairs ends that line of conversation.

Jay is there behind Ryan, along with Atlas and Clay. Miles pulls up the back.

"Chlo! Do we have a game today or what?" Miles calls.

"That's what I'm trying to figure out. I've been sorting your shit out all morning," Chloe says.

"She's always grumpy before breakfast. You want pancakes or French toast?" Jay asks.

"Pancakes," a chorus of voices supplies.

Jay takes the lead. Ryan helps with seriously impressive bacon, and Clay does the toast.

The girls sit around the table, sipping mimosas and coffee while the guys cook. Chloe occasionally rises to try to place a phone call or respond to an email. The guys bring breakfast to the table, setting it around proudly.

When Ryan puts a plate in front of me, leaning close, he says, "Morning."

"Morning."

He's had a shower. His hair is damp, and he smells distractingly delicious.

Did I turn my face toward him to better assess this?

I'm fucked.

"Thanks," I say, my gaze locking with his.

It sounds like I mean for the plate, but really I mean for not saying anything in front of the others.

He tugs a chair in next to me.

As though he's saying he'll keep our secret —for now—but he's not staying away from me.

His hand finds my thigh under the table, his thumb stroking my skin under my shorts.

No one can see it.

I reach for my coffee again.

"I got cars to come pick us up," Chloe announces. "They think they can get through by tonight."

Groans go up.

"What're we going to do about the game?" Atlas grouches.

"LA will dance on our graves," Jay moans.

"Not possible," Ryan weighs in. "They can't record a loss. Tell them to move it."

"Yes, I'll have the league move an entire game date with broadcast deals and ticket sales so we can have our dick-measuring match," Chloe says evenly.

"It's not so bad, you know," Nova says when we're side by side in front of the dishwasher.

"What's not?"

"Dating a Kodiak."

LAST NIGHT, I figured there was some special magic up here. The Christmas spirit edged its way into my grinchy soul.

But the idea that Ryan and I could actually date won't leave my head.

I keep thinking about it all morning: while we clean up breakfast, while I sneak a shower, while we enjoy the last of the cabin.

It's crazy. I'm not looking for a relationship. My life revolves around the bar. Cozy date nights and spilling each other's deepest fears are not on my bingo card.

Not to mention Ryan's experiencing the biggest swoop upward in his young career while I'm wrestling with my own.

Case in point: My dad texted to remind me he had to stock up on beer and to say we can't afford the new lighting fixtures I want to buy.

Which we could if he'd lean on Clay for a moment or let me pay for them.

There's a knock on my door while I'm packing.

Ryan.

He leans a shoulder against the half-open doorway, his eyes full of so much I want him to say and never say all at once. "Chloe not here?"

I turn back to my duffel, setting my makeup bag on top and reaching for the zipper. "I think she's outside on her phone." I slide the zipper closed. "Hopefully you guys will get back in time for the game."

"Don't tell anyone, but I wouldn't be mad if we didn't," he says.

Footsteps at my back have my awareness dialing up. God, I have it bad for this guy.

"I'm sure you could use another day off. You and me both."

Ryan chuckles. "That's not it."

He's close enough to touch me.

Finally, he does.

It's a hand on my arm, but I glance back because I can't resist.

"I'm having too much fun with you."

"With me?" I echo.

"And everyone," he adds as though he thinks I'll slip under his arm and out the door if he comes on too strong.

Maybe I will.

"Come to my game tonight. If we get back."

"I work on Christmas."

"I know. But it would mean a lot to me if you came. You could sit in the team box. Nova and Brooke will be there for sure. Lots of family."

"Yours?"

He shakes his head. "Not this year. One of my sisters has a new baby, so she's not traveling. It would mean even more to have someone there for me."

Damn.

He's thought about this.

"What if we don't get back?" I ask.

"Then spend it with me anyway." His lips tip up. "You might not have much choice, but promise me."

"Okay, I'll go to your game."

"And spend Christmas with me no matter what."

"Fine! I'll spend Christmas with you."

His hand finds my waist, and he tugs me against him. He's so tall I have to press up onto my toes when he kisses me. My hands creep up his chest, reach for the back of his neck, and settle for his shoulders.

"You're too tall," I murmur without lifting my mouth from his.

"You liked it fine last night," he replies the same way.

By the time we break apart, it's been minutes. Perfect, blissful minutes.

He pulls away first. "I better go pack. If I don't leave now, I'm not going to."

I relent and watch him leave, tossing a grin over his shoulder before he reaches the hallway. My heart flips. My stomach too.

I know what I have to do.

I call and get my dad's voicemail. "Dad, it's me. I think I'm going to close the bar tonight."

"I've done it!" Chloe proclaims as she bursts in the front door half an hour later, filling the entire cabin with her voice. "I am a queen. A goddess. All should bow down."

I'm padding back downstairs and wondering if anyone would notice if Ryan and I disappeared to the loft for a while.

"What happened?" Brooke asks, looking up from where she's reading a magazine in an overstuffed chair.

"The road is open. SUVs with chains are arriving anytime. We're getting back in time for the game."

Cheers go up, Atlas pumping his fists in the air and Miles and Jay high-fiving.

The guys are competitive, and they don't want to miss their chance to beat LA. Plus, missing the game would disappoint the fans.

"The team will go first, and we'll follow," Chloe's saying.

We pile bags and bins by the door. Taking down the Christmas decorations feels bittersweet.

"I'm kind of bummed we have to take this down," I confide in Nova.

"I know. But the game will be great. I never used to get playing a sport on Christmas, but it's pretty fun. You're coming, right?"

"Yeah, I guess I am."

Her face brightens with delight before she loops an arm through mine. "We're going to have the best time. I love the ugly holiday sweaters they give out. You probably have a bunch of them."

"Actually, I don't have any."

"You don't have one?" Ryan overhears and swoops in. He shakes his head. "We're going to fix that today."

A banging outside has us looking over.

"That must be the car!" Jay's already heading for the door, Ryan on his heels.

Jay jams his feet into his boots and is outside the next second. We rush to follow, all of us in a pile that spills out onto the porch.

Jay stops at once, lifting his arms. "Oh shit."

There's a new addition to the clearing in front of the house, paused and watchful.

It's not an SUV.

It's a bear.

17

———

SIERRA

The bear studies us for a breath, two. It's not even ten feet away, its dark fur shiny.

Then it lets out a roar.

I jump. There's no avoiding the reaction, because if there's a way to respond to a wild animal with claws and teeth surprising you, I don't know what it is.

"Aren't they supposed to be hibernating?" Ryan murmurs.

"Tell that to the bear," I whisper.

That's when I realize the bear isn't as big as others I've seen from a distance, or on TV. It's probably young—a year or two old.

Our crew inches closer together, either by design or instinct.

"What kind is it?" Atlas asks.

Clay leans in. "Black bear."

"Obviously," Jay weighs in.

After a moment, it drops down to all fours and watches us.

It's come here for food, and it isn't ready to leave, but maybe it's decided that it's over-matched by this cluster of mostly-oversized humans.

"We should make a lot of noise. Scare it off," Brooke whispers.

We all look at Atlas, who lifts his arms in the air and growls.

The bear sniffs but doesn't move away. I'd say its expression is more expectant than aggressive.

"Does it think...?" Ryan starts.

"What?" Jay asks.

"Does it know we're bears too?" he finishes.

A scuffling and snorting creature behind us cuts through the crowd toward the parking lot.

"Waffles, no!" Brooke calls too late.

The Frenchie rushes to the front of our

group, pulling up almost comically fast. He tips his face up and yips.

The bear lowers its face.

"Waffles…" Brooke lunges for the dog, and Jay grabs her.

Another sound comes from the woods.

The bear turns and ambles away.

"Its mom?" I ask.

"It was too old for that. Too young for a mate."

"So, who was it looking out for? Bears don't travel in packs," Jay insists.

Miles cuts him a look. "Whatever you say, Nat Geo."

We all slump against one another. Brooke runs forward to collect Waffles, scooping him into her arms and telling him they need to have a talk.

I'm leaning on Ryan, his heart thudding under my ear.

A black car roof appears between the pine trees lining the drive, then a second one.

"There's our ride. Everyone, finish packing," Chloe directs. "Team will go in the two black cars. We can drive ourselves."

"Too dangerous," Clay says.

"It's fine," Chloe says. "I've got snow tires on my car and—"

"You want to risk your neck, that's your business. But my wife isn't driving back herself. Ladies, take the other SUV."

"It's going to be a clown car with the five of you," Nova warns.

"Worth it."

The other guys nod in agreement, except Atlas, who knows better than to say anything.

Chloe relents, and we all disperse to collect our things. I load my stuff into the back of one SUV.

The adrenaline is still pounding in my veins from the bear when my phone rings.

"Dad. Hi," I answer as I squish my duffel atop Brooke's designer luggage.

"Sierra, honey. Got your message. Everything okay?"

I readjust the angle so the hatchback can close. "There's been a ton of snow up here. We're trying to get home."

"If you won't be back in time to open, I'll go in."

"No, I think I'll be back." I step back, admiring my handiwork as Ryan emerges and loads his bag into the other car. "It's just... I have somewhere else I want to be tonight."

I watch Ryan's fluid movements, admiring. I can't wait to watch him from the Kodiaks' box, and after... we can do everything we did last night and more.

"Mile High can't close tonight." Dad's voice brings me back to earth. "We've been open every Christmas for twenty years."

I rip my gaze from Ryan, blinking as I pace the treeline. "It's Christmas, Dad. Can't they live without their Miller Lites for one night?"

He sighs. "Honey, I know you have friends on that team, but we're not like them. We don't get nights off. We keep the lights on."

Ryan

"That's the last of it?"

"Thank fuck. There's no way we're all going to fit," Jay says under his breath.

"Get cozy. It is the season."

"Was that the best pre-Christmas getaway or what?" I say proudly.

"Stranded at a cabin, weird gift exchange, almost got eaten by a bear," Atlas lists off deadpan.

"I wouldn't say we almost got eaten," Miles weighs in.

I wait them out. "So?"

"It was good, Rookie," Clay decides.

The other guys grudgingly agree.

"But you're still doing media for a month."

I throw up my hands, but honestly, I can live with that.

It's Christmas.

We're going to be home in time for the game.

The girl I've been into for forever finally admitted she's going to give it a try.

Things are looking up.

Sierra taps me on the shoulder as I'm about to shift into the car. "Hey. Can I talk to you for a sec?"

"Sure."

The guys are locked in a conversation about how to arrange their legs, so I step outside and shut the door behind me.

"I'll make sure you get a killer seat tonight." I grin. "VIP treatment for my lucky charm."

She doesn't smile. Instead, she looks a little sick.

I'm instantly concerned. "What's up?"

"I can't come to the game tonight."

As fast as my mood had risen, it crashes. "Why not?"

She shoves her hands in her back pockets. "I have to work."

"You can take one night off. It's not that hard."

"Maybe for you. You have a huge contract. The world isn't the same for you as it is for me." She looks around, past me. "This was a bad idea."

My stomach drops like a chunk of wet snow falling out of a tree branch and splatting on the ground.

I've wanted this girl for as long as I can remember. Always watched her out the corner of my eye. Wanted to make her smile.

Just because I'm young doesn't mean I don't know what I want.

The back door of the SUV cracks open. "Hey, Ryan!" Jay hollers. "We've got a game to get to."

I'm still staring at Sierra.

I shut the door again and turn back to the woman who's completely thrown me. She looks as though she'd rather be anywhere but facing me right now.

"Is there anything I can say to change your mind?"

She wraps her arms around her, her mouth falling open as if the idea of me trying is ludicrous. "No. Have a good Christmas, Ryan."

It takes everything in me to reach for the door of the SUV and pretend nothing happened.

18

SIERRA

"Merry Christmas, Sierra!" One of our regulars lifts his glass to me.

"You too, Pete."

Mile High is bustling as the game comes on. Every one of the half dozen TVs is tuned to the stadium right down the road where the Kodiaks are getting ready to host LA.

"Your dad said you might not get back."

"It was pretty close," I admit as I refill the ice in the tray in front of me.

Pete laughs. "It's the holiday, and there's a game. That's all I care about. As long as we beat LA."

Pete turns back to his friends, all wearing jerseys. One of the guys has a Santa hat.

The words remind me of what my dad said. They're not here for me.

My chest feels hollow.

The past couple of days were amazing, but that's not my world. Just like I got swept up in the holiday spirit, I got swept up in Ryan.

On the screen, the announcers finish their pregame remarks, and the broadcast cuts to the team intros.

LA is out first, jogging onto the court to hollers from the home crowd I can see but not hear because of the muted TVs.

Next is our team.

The crowd is on its feet—mostly Denver fans wearing purple holiday sweaters. This is everyone's idea of the best time. I was listening to stories on the radio earlier of how people got tickets and what they did to get them.

The Kodiaks' starters appear one by one.

Atlas with a one-handed wave to the crowd, his eyes cool and focused.

Miles, running and tilting his head to one side then the other.

Jay, clapping to get him into the headspace.

Ryan.

My heart skips as he trots onto the court.

Is he as distracted as I am?

I analyze his tilted chin and smile to acknowledge the crowd.

I could be in the box right now with my friends.

But I have to look out for myself. If we tried and failed, I'd not only feel like a total idiot, but it would risk screwing up everything I've worked for here.

I glance around to see where the patrons' attention is directed, then discreetly turn the nearest TV to another channel.

A couple of people protest. "Sierra! What're you doing?"

"It's on the other five," I remind them, pointing at the next closest screen.

Flicking through channels, I settle on Nat Geo. Some bunnies are playing in the forest.

Good. Bunnies are good.

I throw myself into work, pouring beers and mixing the occasional cocktail.

It works pretty well, until the bar erupts with cheers when the Kodiaks score or boos when LA does.

After the first quarter, the Kodiaks are up by a little.

"Did you see that play?" Pete taps the bar excitedly. "Ryan's going to be the next franchise player."

"He's earning his keep, but I wouldn't go that far," one of his friends counters.

"What do you think, Sierra?"

The bottle of whisky under the bar is calling my name.

It's not clear whether a drink of it would clear my head of Ryan or make me remember the times we were together.

I ignore the bottle and force myself to watch the replay: Jay moves down the court with the ball, Miles streaks toward the perimeter for a three, Jay fakes passing to Miles and goes instead to Ryan, who cuts toward the basket for a dunk.

"I think he loves the game and this town and we'd be lucky to have him," I say.

During halftime, I appreciate the relief of not having Ryan on the screen every second.

"Sierra?"

I look up to see a courier in a Santa hat

holding a purple-wrapped package with a red bow. "I didn't order anything."

"It's a gift. Can you please sign?"

I reluctantly comply, thanking the guy, and set the package on the bar.

"What is it?" Pete demands.

"I know what comes in that paper!" one of his friends says.

"I'm not opening it."

"You have to!" the guys insist. "It's Christmas!"

I wipe down the bar so everything is extra clean, then I take out the card.

"FOR MY FAVORITE GRINCH. *So I can be with you in spirit. — R*"

MY FINGERS ITCH as I tug the bow loose and open the beautiful paper.

Inside is a purple sweater.

"Ugly Christmas sweater!" the guys chorus.

"What's on the back?" Pete prods, nodding toward the sweater.

I turn the hoodie over, and my breath lodges in my throat.

It's Ryan's jersey number.

Hollers go up.

"They haven't ever done one player before." Pete turns to his friend. "Have they?"

"Let me check. A guy from my work got tickets to the game." He sends off a text.

My stomach flips over, my hand stroking the numbers on the hoodie.

"Ahah! That's not the sweater. It has 'Merry Bearmas' on it." He holds up a photo on the screen. "So, how'd you get a Ryan one?"

Damn it.

It didn't cost him anything ridiculous, I remind myself. He's loaded and could order a thousand with the snap of his fingers. *But he wants you wearing his name.*

It's easy for a guy to claim a girl as his when he doesn't have to be hers too.

He's trying to mess with me. Except... that's not his style. Every moment he's ever been with me, he's been genuine.

"It's an inside joke, I guess." I set it under the bar carefully, next to the whisky.

The next time I look up, the rabbits are gone.

Instead, there's a bear.

Then a few of them.

Subtitles appear at the bottom of the screen, where the narrator explains how bear siblings often look out for each other even after they leave their parents. Sometimes they even adopt new bears as their own.

I'm a lone wolf, but that doesn't mean I want to be forever.

I could be part of this group.

With Ryan, I feel as though I don't need to become someone different, or prove myself, or blend in, or hell—even stand out.

The second half starts, and I reluctantly turn my Nat Geo TV back to the Kodiaks right as they do a close-up on Ryan.

I take a deep breath and exhale. I know what I need to do.

"Guys, as soon as the game is over, I'm closing."

19

RYAN

If you've never seen thirty thousand people in matching Christmas sweaters on their feet and hollering, you've never lived.

The floor is shaking, my eardrums pulsing with the noise from the crowd. The ball goes up against our net, and I catch it off the rim.

Ten seconds.

Adrenaline pounds in my veins as I throw it forward to Jay, who's almost at center court. I run up after him, and he brings it over the line and passes it back to me.

The final seconds of the game tick down, and I sneak a glance at the scoreboard. Satisfaction roots in my chest. I dribble out the final seconds, LA pulling up because they know they've lost.

The ref blows the whistle, but it's impossible to hear in the deafening arena. I toss him the ball.

"Only pie they're gonna be eating is the humble kind!" Jay hollers as he fist-bumps me.

Even Clay is grinning, and the guy has seen it all.

A few of the LA guys come up, and we trade hugs and fist bumps. It's the holiday after all.

Denver won. On Christmas Day.

Against one of our biggest rivals.

I used to dream of these moments as a kid, but living it for real...

There's no better feeling.

Except that even as red-and-purple streamers flutter from the ceiling, the media descends on the court for the post-game interviews, and everyone is in an objectively jovial mood, something's missing.

I feel it through the on-court interviews, TV personalities wanting to know if it's easier or harder to play on a holiday.

It's there when I make my way back to the dressing room and I hit the shower.

Definitely there when I grab my phone in my locker to find it blowing up with messages from family and friends.

Probably because I'm thinking of one person who's not in my phone.

Sierra.

She should have been here. I pictured it in my head, was so damn happy when she said yes. But she's not. She pulled away, and whatever shot I had is over.

"You're onto something with this Christmas cabin," Jay says, pulling his phone and gear out of his locker. "We should make it a tradition."

"Yeah. I'll see what I can do," I say, but I'm distracted.

"We're all going back to Clay's," Miles is saying, but I'm tuning him out.

The past few days felt almost as good as being home for the holidays. It was spending time with the guys, but it was also her.

My phone rings with a video call. My parents.

My heart lifts a little.

I answer but put my thumb over the camera.

"Merry Christmas!" they chorus.

My sisters are there. Cousins and aunts and uncles too.

"What's wrong with your video?" one of my sisters demands.

"I'm in the locker room so can't put you on video."

"A bunch of sweaty naked guys?"

"Is Clay there?" my other sister asks. "I will give you everything I own if you put on video."

They laugh and I grin, tossing a look at my teammate who's changing.

I feel right at home here. I'm missing my family, but I have another one with these guys.

"We need to go check on the turkey," my mom says, capturing the phone and taking me with her. "What's wrong, honey? It's just us."

"Nothing." I take my thumb off the camera as she walks.

"I know you. You play tough, but you have a soft heart."

I sigh. "There's this girl I'm really into. But she's not willing to go there with me, and I don't want to be that guy to drag her for it. She has people telling her what they want from her all the time."

Mom's eyes shine with understanding.

"Then tell her what you want to give her instead."

"And if she still doesn't want it?"

"Her loss, honey."

Funny. It feels like mine.

Voices drift into the kitchen alongside my mom's. My cousins are arguing about the dessert.

"Are you on video now?!" one demands. "Is Clay there?!"

A message comes in, capturing my attention.

Sierra: Great game.

"Thanks, Mom. I gotta go," I say quickly. "Call you later?"

She agrees despite the protests behind her, and I say goodbye and hang up.

My heart is thudding as if I'm still on the court as I type back.

Ryan: Thanks. You've never texted me before.

Sierra: I promised I'd text you after we hooked up this time. So, Merry Christmas.

My chest warms, my hands tingling.

"Be good to her. She's been through a lot."

Clay's gruff voice has me looking up.

"What do you mean?"

"Mile High's been through some rough times. Dragged Sierra and her family with it. It's doing better now, but when you're used to giving your all to something, it's hard to think about anything else, not to mention trust it."

I don't ask him how he knows, because it doesn't matter. I believe him.

That won't happen with me.

I have to prove it to her.

THE SIGN on the door says "Closed," but there are still patrons inside Mile High when I make my way through the snowy streets and park close by the bar. The warm lights inside can't quash the nerves in my stomach as I adjust the stuffed Christmas bear under my arm and push my way inside.

Jingle bells over the door tinkle brightly.

"We're closing," Sierra calls without turning around.

"Damn it. I was hoping to get a drink."

Then she does turn. Her eyes widen in slow motion. "Ryan."

The other patrons recognize me instantly and call my name. A few guys clap me on the back, and I nod and smile, but I'm focused on only one person.

I cross the room, stopping opposite the bar and taking in her outfit. "I like your sweater."

"Thanks."

There's too much space between us.

I round the bar.

"What're you...?"

I pull up right in front of her. "I've been into you for a long time."

She bites her lip, looking up at me with wariness and maybe a sliver of hope.

It's hard to stay focused when she's so beautiful, but I need to say my piece.

"When last year happened, I thought that was it. That was my shot. And for sure you'd text me after we hooked up." There's a holler from behind me, one of the guys overhearing what I said. Shit, too late to take it back. "Then you didn't, and I figured you needed time. Then we were on the road, and it was a month, and two months, and then it was too late.

"It's not like I hit on you thinking I wanted more. Hell, I didn't even hit on you thinking I wanted sex. It just happened. And because I liked you—more than I could admit—I didn't want to be some asshole who texted you because I'm sure you have a million losers blowing up your phone..." I go to shove a hand through my hair and realize I've got my Santa hat on. "You obviously had my number because you're in the group chats. So, I figured you forgot all about me."

There's silence behind me. The patrons must have left.

There's mistletoe hanging over the bar.

"You're kind of hard to forget, Ryan," she says at last.

A smidgeon of hope blooms in my chest.

"Because you work at a bar with my jersey on the wall?" I ask.

She inhales. "Because every time the Kodiaks come in here, I look for you."

"Awww," erupts behind us.

She looks past me. "Pete! I mean it. We're closing."

"Come on, Sierra. This is better than the game!" he pleads, his friends nodding and clutching their hands together.

"Go," she says firmly, pointing at the door.

They head outside, dragging their feet. She follows and shuts the door behind them.

They're staring through the window when she returns to me, and I know she knows because she rolls her eyes.

"I know you're afraid it'll mess with your vibe to date a Kodiak, but I'll do everything in my power to make your life better and not worse," I say. "We can take it slow if that's what you need, but we have to start somewhere. And I really want to go somewhere with you, Sierra."

Her eyes flicker with vulnerability.

For a second, I wonder if she's going to put distance between us, but she returns to the spot she was in before, inches in front of me.

"When you invited me up to the cabin for Christmas, I was a little too excited." Sierra's lips part. Fuck, I want to kiss her so badly, but I need to hear what she has to say. "I hate Christmas."

"I love that about you."

She sighs. "What I mean is, I told myself it was a bad idea to entertain the idea of letting myself be into you. My entire world revolves around you and the team, and that's a harsh reality. But you make me question things I thought I knew. And all I could think was, why should some rookie with magic hands change me?"

I hold up a hand. "One, I was rookie of the year. Two... I'd like to get the magic hands part in writing."

Sierra shakes her head at either my words or my shit-eating grin. Eventually, she smiles too.

"Well, we have more in common than you think. My world kind of revolves around you too."

Her mouth falls open as though she can't believe I said that.

"Did you rehearse that part?" she whispers.

"Nope." My throat works. "Guess I'm feeling inspired."

She steps closer. "By the holiday season?"

"By how good you look in that sweater."

"You think?" She spins, and I get a chance

to see my number on her. All the blood goes straight to my dick.

I'm picturing bending her over this bar and flipping up her skirt, fucking her like this so I know she's mine.

Don't get distracted.

I turn her back to face me.

"This part I did rehearse." I take a deep breath. "I get that you have this story about who you are. And you have one about me too." Her eyes widen as I take her face in my palms. "I can't say I don't care who you are or what you do. That I don't care you run your dad's bar. That you're suspicious of guys, especially exceptionally attractive ones."

Her eyes narrow, and she starts to tug back. I don't let her.

"But I love all those things about you. And I would fucking love it if you gave us a chance."

The moment stretches out between us. Now that I've declared my feelings, I can imagine everything she might say.

That I'm being impulsive. That I don't know what I want.

It's all bullshit. I won't let her go if there's a chance she could stay.

She folds her arms, never breaking my gaze.

"What do you say, Sierra? Will you date me this Christmas?"

"Only for Christmas?" Her head tilts playfully.

"And New Year's. And Valentine's Day. And if it's going well… Easter. Easter is my favorite."

"I thought Christmas was your favorite."

"I'm a man of layers."

"Kiss him!" the guy she called Pete exclaims through the window.

Sierra tips her face up. "I guess that's what the mistletoe is for."

"Damn right it is."

Then I kiss her and cheers go up.

Those are all the holiday vibes I need.

EPILOGUE
SIERRA

"Busy night," Julie comments as we cross paths behind the bar.

"Fridays are the busiest."

Our dance is a well-practiced routine that keeps us filling beer pints and pitchers from the taps of local brews and mixing the occasional cocktail. It keeps me fresh.

We're both going full tilt, serving the happy patrons who watched the game here, not to mention the overflow we'll get once fans flood out of the stadium and over to the bar in about twenty minutes. Mile High does a good business, win or lose. Lately, there've been a lot of wins.

"The team's on a hot streak since January," I toss back.

"Which has nothing to do with you."

I roll my eyes. "I'm a humble bartender."

"You're not humble. The other part is true."

We both laugh.

"There you boys go." I drop off an order for Pete and his friends.

"This the new one?" He lifts the glass and turns it. "Nice color."

"It's great. A local brewery. We only have it for a limited time."

"So don't get hooked," he jokes.

I lean a hip against the side of their booth. "That's what Dad said. But vote with your wallet, and if you love it, we'll get more where that came from." I point at the poster on the wall with our list of newly rotating taps from local microbreweries.

The doors open and a group sweeps in wearing jerseys. The start of the game crowd.

It feels good, the energy.

My dad agreed to let me have more rein with the bar. I recently went on a trip to Miami to check out some bars there for inspiration.

I go back behind the bar and keep working.

"Sorry we're late!" Nova exclaims as she and Brooke drop onto two empty stools. "The guys are on their way. Ryan was extra popular in media, and Chloe's looking out for him."

"Never apologize," I say and mean it. "How are you feeling?" I glance at her stomach, the discreet baby bump that's starting to show.

"Great. As for our excuse, traffic was brutal, but we're going to make it up to you. We have big news."

I pause to lean over the bar. "Tell me."

Brooke folds her hands and crosses one leg over the other. "I finally picked a designer for the wedding."

"Wow! Congrats." I cut a look at Nova. "Was that harder or easier than choosing a groom?"

Brooke laughs.

It's good to see them doing well. Lately, I've been busy at the bar but also spending more time with the girls.

A cheer erupts that fills the entirety of Mile High.

The Kodiaks are here.

Jay is first, with Clay. Then Miles and a couple of the bench guys. Atlas and Ryan bring up the back.

Jay waves to me, and I nod back because my hands are full. I smile, my head bobbing to the music.

"Nice game," I call as they approach.

"Thanks. It was touch-and-go there until Miles decided to show up in the second half."

"I was lulling them into complacency," Miles says.

"I had to shake them out of it." Ryan shifts between them with a grin. He's gorgeous. After the game, he's freshly showered, his dark, curly hair damp. "Hey, Sierra."

"Hi." I can handle myself. Just because a starting guard on the world champion Kodiaks is looking at me as if he's starved and I'm a steak doesn't mean I'll break.

"Catch much of the game?"

"Not much. It's been a busy night." Since I introduced a new cocktail list, we're getting a broader clientele. Everyone is still focused on the team, but we're pulling in younger fans, more women too.

"I'll reenact it for you."

"Yeah, yeah. Keep it in your pants," Jay pleads, and the other guys laugh.

A group of vaguely familiar women wedges

its way in front of the bar, cutting in front of the crowd.

Kodashians. I can tell from their swag.

In the front is a blonde with huge boobs.

She looks vaguely familiar.

I search my memory for a second, then another.

Oh no. It's Cherry Girl, the one who gave me the insanely hard time over missing her favorite garnish.

"Tequila Sunrise," she requests.

Her friend picks up a menu off the bar, scanning the cocktail list. "Do you still have the Rookie Season? It's not on the menu, but—"

"That was only a Christmas drink, wasn't it?" one of her friends asks.

"It's here year-round."

Their heads snap up as they clock Ryan a few feet down the bar, where he's claimed a seat next to Atlas and Jay.

"We're still deciding if it's seasonal," I inform Ryan.

"But between us, it's going to stay," Ryan tells them.

God, he's obnoxious. The confident ease.

"It is, is it?" I plant both hands on my hips.

His gaze flicks back to me and lingers, his expression saying every second he's not looking at me might be a waste. He sizes me up from the toes of my boots to the tip of my ponytail. Then he gets off his seat and rounds the bar.

I throw up both hands. "Excuse me, do I come to your work and get up on the court?!"

The Kodiaks laugh, and the girls watch, seemingly fascinated.

But Ryan ignores them and comes closer. "Are you kidding? I'd love to see it. Maybe you can wear my jersey."

"What are you doing?" I demand when he pulls up an inch from me. I have to crane my neck to meet his eyes.

His hand finds my waist, his thumb brushing my ribcage familiarly as he leans closer. "Making sure you know that drink isn't going anywhere." He lowers his voice to murmur in my ear, "Like me."

It's two words, but my entire body rebels against every sensible instinct I have.

The rookie I hooked up with isn't a rookie, and we're dating, not hooking up.

Not that we're *not* hooking up. I have a lip-bitingly filthy reel of things we've done and places we've done it, matched only by the list of ones I still want to try.

In the three months since Christmas, we've gone from seeing one another twice a week at Mile High to spending most of our free seconds together. It's hard, given how much I work and his travel schedule, but we're both committed to making it work.

If Ryan was the perfect hookup, he's even better as a boyfriend: attentive, funny, caring. When we disagree, he's a better communicator than I am. Maybe from being raised by women.

Speaking of, I've met his parents and sisters, and they're the best. Their vibe as a bigger family is mesmerizing, and I love watching him banter with them.

I've also inherited a whole new family in the Kodiaks—one I realize now I was already part of but never embraced completely.

My dad is a little starstruck. There's nothing he'd like better than me dating a member of his favorite team, but he's been remarkably chill about it around my new boyfriend, which I appreciate.

"Dammit, Ryan," I murmur when his grip

on me only tightens. "I'm trying to run a business, and people need their drinks." I wave past him, expecting a line of impatient customers.

Instead, everyone's enjoying the show. The Kodiaks are laughing and nodding. Brooke's giving me an "I told you so" look, and Nova's eyes are misty.

Even Pete and his friends are watching with goofy smiles.

God. We're like a rom-com.

Except for Cherry Girl. She looks as though she ate an entire cherry, pit and all.

"I get it, you're embarrassed to do this here..." Ryan starts.

I grab the back of his head and pull him down to me. He kisses me back, and cheers fill the bar one more time.

I guess the holidays aren't so bad after all.

Thank you for reading *Rookie Season*! I hope you loved spending more time with Ryan, Sierra and the Denver Kodiaks.

Sign up for Piper Lawson's newsletter to get free books, exclusive deals and more.

Join today at:
www.piperlawsonbooks.com/subscribe

Plus, if you missed it, Clay and Nova's complete story—the romance that started it all!—is available now in the King of the Court series.

Love,

Piper

BOOKS BY PIPER LAWSON

FOR A FULL LIST PLEASE GO TO
PIPERLAWSONBOOKS.COM/BOOKS

KING OF THE COURT SERIES

I'm king of the court. There's no room in my life for a queen.

A steamy, grumpy sunshine sports romance featuring a woman down on her luck, a star basketball player with a filthy mouth, and a connection neither of them can deny.

DENVER KODIAKS SERIES

It's not every day you ask your older brother's teammate to be your fake boyfriend. But desperate times call for gorgeous, impulsive measures.

A steamy, brother's teammate sports romance about a sorority reunion, a college crush, and a love that's bigger than basketball.

WICKED SERIES

Rockstars don't chase college students. But Jax Jamieson never followed the rules.

A new adult rock star series full of nerdy girls, hot

rock stars, pet skunks, and ensemble casts you'll want to be friends with forever.

RIVALS SERIES

At seventeen, I offered Tyler Adams my home, my life, my heart. He stole them all.

An angsty new adult series. Fans of forbidden romance, enemies to lovers, friends to lovers, and rock star romance will love these books.

ENEMIES SERIES

I sold my soul to a man I hate. Now, he owns me.

An enthralling, explosive romance about an American DJ and a British billionaire. If you like wealthy, royal alpha males, enemies to lovers, travel or sexy romance, this series is for you!

OFF-LIMITS SERIES

Turns out the beautiful man from the club is my new professor... But he wasn't when he kissed me.

A forbidden age gap college romance series. Find out what happens when the beautiful man from the club is Olivia's hot new professor.

TRAVESTY SERIES

My best friend's brother grew up. Hot.

A steamy romance series following best friends who start a fashion label from NYC to LA. It contains best friends brother, second chances, enemies to lovers, opposites attract and friends to lovers stories. If you like sexy, sassy romances, you'll love this series.

PLAY SERIES

I know what I want. It's not Max Donovan. To hell with his money, his gaming empire, and his joystick.

An addictive series of standalone romances with slow burn tension, delicious banter, office romance and unforgettable characters. If you like smart, quirky, steamy enemies-to-lovers, contemporary romance, you'll love Play.

MODERN ROMANCE SERIES

When your rich, handsome best friend asks you to be his fake girlfriend? Say no.

A smart, sexy series of contemporary romances following a set of female friends running a relationship marketing company in NYC. If you enjoy hot guys who treat their families like gold, fun antics, dirty talk, real characters, steamy scenes, badass heroines and smart banter, you'll love this series.

ABOUT THE AUTHOR

Piper Lawson is a *Wall Street Journal* and *USA Today* bestselling author of smart and steamy romance.

She writes women who follow their dreams, best friends who know your dirty secrets and love you anyway, and complex heroes you'll fall hard for.

Piper lives in Canada with her tall and brilliant husband. She's a sucker for dark eyes, dark coffee, and dark chocolate.

For a complete reading list, visit
www.piperlawsonbooks.com/books

Subscribe to Piper's VIP email list
www.piperlawsonbooks.com/subscribe

amazon.com/author/piperlawson

bookbub.com/authors/piper-lawson

instagram.com/piperlawsonbooks

tiktok.com/@piperlawsonbooks

facebook.com/piperlawsonbooks

goodreads.com/piperlawson

ACKNOWLEDGMENTS

Thank you for reading *Rookie Season*! I hope this holiday novella gave you all the cozy feels.

This was my first time writing a holiday story but it won't be my last! I loved channeling all the celebratory vibes into this snowed-in snack.

This book wouldn't have happened without the support of my awesome readers, including my ARC readers. Thank you for providing endless enthusiasm, cheerleading, early feedback, and help spreading the word.

Thank you to my editors Cassie Robertson and Devon Burke; to my team Kate Tilton and Annette Brignac; to my designer Najla Qamber; and to the team at Valentine PR. Thank you all for your wisdom, enthusiasm and tireless effort to help readers find books they'll love.

Last but not least, thank YOU for reading. Truly. Knowing we're living in these words and worlds together is the best part of any gig I've ever had.

Love always,
Piper

www.ingramcontent.com/pod-product-compliance
Lightning Source LLC
Chambersburg PA
CBHW061246310726
48971CB00007B/2239